Perfect Lies

By G W Gresham

This is a work of fiction. names, characters, places and incidents are the product of the author's imagination or are used fictitiously. Any resemblance to actual events, locales, or persons living or dead is purely coincidental.

ISBN 0-9841701-0-3
www.gwgresham.com

1

THE GOVERNOR WALKED out to the pool and saw the reflections dancing from the light blue water. Steam rose and disappeared quickly into the cool night air. He laid his glasses down and dove into the warm water.

The water sizzled when he met it, and by the time he surfaced, he felt like he was cooking in hot grease. The smells of his own burning flesh filled his nostrils. His skin split open and blood mixed with the water. He desperately tried to yell but nothing came out of his mouth, already deformed.

He tried to pull himself out of the pool but had no strength. He fell back in the water and his skin and muscle fell off of his bones and sank to the bottom. The pool consumed him so quick, in a matter of minutes; not even his bones remained.

The black limousine pulled in front of the Wentworth building, and Martin Wentworth admired his creation. The forty floors of gold tinted glass looked like it belonged at the end of the rainbow.

The uniformed driver quickly got out and opened the rear door.

Martin's custom-made alligator cowboy boots hit the ground and his large frame rose to its six foot two height. His two hundred and twenty-pound body filled out his western cut suit. He finished his look off with a 100 X beaver cowboy hat.

He smiled at the thought of making his mark on the world, and at age fifty-six, still had a lot more years to enjoy it.

He loved the power his money gave him, but like so many self-made men, it was not only the money, but the game that was important too.

The two uniformed attendants opened the ten-foot, double glass doors when Martin stepped close.

He carried a designer briefcase in his left hand and shook each of their hands with his right. "Dean, how are you doin'?"

"I'm just fine, Mr. Wentworth. How are you today, sir?"

"I'm rich, Dean. How in the hell do you think I am?"

"Yes, sir." Dean laughed.

"Good morning, Mr. Wentworth." The second young man smiled at him.

Martin looked him up and down once. "I don't believe I know you, son."

"I'm Cody Thomas. It's my pleasure to meet you, sir."

"Cody Thomas?" Martin was surprised. "Didn't you play pro ball for Dallas?"

"A few years back before my knee blew out."

"So what are you doing here?"

"Gotta' make a living, sir."

"Well I'll have to see if I can find a more suitable job for you. I'll have my assistant look into it and contact you."

"Thank you, Mr. Wentworth." The young man looked pleased.

Martin took off his hat and entered the lobby. He walked directly toward an attractive, blond woman behind the magazine counter. She looked especially good today.

"Doris, I swear you get prettier every time I see you. Darlin', how are you?"

She smiled when she saw him. "Good morning, Mr. Wentworth. I'm just fine and you?"

"Well, I'm always better when I see your bright little face to start my day off. It's a good thing I'm a married man, sweetheart. Otherwise, you and I would be an item."

"Mr. Wentworth, I love it when you stop by and see me. Can I offer you the morning paper today?"

"Genuine Southern hospitality. I love that, and I will take a paper from you. Just do me a favor and don't ever change." Martin reached in his pocket and gave the woman a hundred-dollar bill. When she saw the money, he gestured to her not to say anything. He winked at her, walked away, and got into the elevator.

Martin took a gold card from his jacket pocket and inserted it into the control panel. The card gave him access to the private offices on the upper floors of the building.

The elevator reached the thirty-seventh floor and the doors opened to a long hallway.

Martin walked out a door that opened to an outside terrace that over looked downtown Houston.

On Martin's left, a man sat at a patio table wearing an expensive Italian suit. He smoked a cigarette and drank coffee.

Martin's older brother, Matthew, sat with the man and the sweet smell of his Cuban cigar consumed the air.

Martin smiled at the two men as he approached them.

"This must be the smoking section." He reached out and shook hands with the man in the Italian suit.

"Mr. Wentworth, it's my pleasure to see you, sir," he said, and stood up.

"Austin, the pleasure is mine. I can't tell you how pleased I am with your work. The situation with the governor turned out as perfect as I expected." Martin sat down at the table with the two men.

Matthew poured him a cup of coffee and pushed it over to him.

Martin pulled an envelope out of his jacket pocket and set it in front of Austin. "The amount we discussed and a little bonus for a job well done. I continue to be impressed with the flawless and discreet work you do."

"Thank you, Mr. Wentworth," Austin said. He picked up the envelope and put it in his jacket pocket.

"You do get creative, Austin, I'll give you that." Martin drank his coffee.

"The acid not only kills but disposes of any evidence. A trick I learned when I worked for the CIA."

"Well, it took care of our problem. I'll be in touch again soon."

Austin shook hands with Martin and disappeared through a door in the building.

Martin and Matthew went through another door and walked down a hallway filled with offices. They opened twelve-foot double doors into Martin's luxurious office and walked in.

It looked like the Houston skyline occupied the room with them. Large windows surrounded them and splashed a spectacular view of tall, office buildings.

Pictures of Martin smiling with a number of American Presidents hung on the walls along with the many awards his company, Texmar, had received.

Western sculptures rested on pedestals built into the walls and were lit by recessed lights.

Martin sat in a brown, leather chair behind a massive, solid oak desk. He picked up the phone, and punched a button. "Susie, would you hold my calls for a few minutes, darlin'?" He smiled and hung up the phone.

Matthew sat in a chair in front of Martin's desk.

Martin's son, Marty, walked in the office and closed the tall doors behind him. He smiled at his father and handed him a folded piece of paper.

"It seems as though the governor of the great state of Texas is missing, gentleman. Doesn't that just break you all up? Lieutenant Governor Simms is being sworn in as we speak. That means our project in the gulf can be started back up immediately. You've gotta' love a politician who takes your money?" Martin said smiling at his brother, Matthew.

Matthew breathed out a sigh of relief. "It's gonna" be nice without him for a change. We'll make more money than we could ever imagine with Simms in office."

Marty fixed drinks at the bar. "I think we should have hung him from the flagpole at the capitol. His staff could have found him in the morning."

Martin chuckled at his son's comment. "I suppose you would have drug the man through the streets first?"

Marty rolled his eyes. "I wish you would have let me handle it. For all of the trouble he caused us, he should have suffered more."

Martin took the drink from Marty. "This will be a profitable year for us, gentlemen. Texmar is about to take a giant step forward." Martin raised his glass for a toast. "Here's to the new governor of the great state of Texas. Gentlemen, we now have total control over this state."

2

AT NINE A.M. the temperature had already reached seventy degrees in Southern California. Cole Tyler arrived at Tyler Transport and pulled his black, Mercedes SL into the presidents parking spot. While he walked inside the building, his general manager, Derek Lane, saw him.

"Hey buddy," Derek said, as they both entered the elevator. "How did your weekend go? By the look you're giving me, I'd say you and Jan aren't getting along again. Would you like to talk about it?"

Cole punched the forth floor button and the doors closed. "Well, it's not too complicated. She wants a more permanent relationship and I want to keep things simple. We talked about this when we first got together, but I guess things change."

"Tell me about it, Crystal put me through hell when she wanted to get married. She had this way of shutting me out when she wanted something. I don't even like to think about it."

"You seem happy with her," Cole said.

"I couldn't imagine living without her. When you find the right person, life is good. You just need to find the right girl, buddy."

"Well, I suppose I can't be single all my life. I'm sure one day I'll meet the right girl." Cole looked at the morning paper. "Can you believe this about the Governor of Texas? His swimming pool had so much acid in it there was nothing left of him to bury."

"He messed with the wrong guy," Derek said.

The elevator reached the fourth floor and the doors opened into a large office with several cubicles scattered around the room.

An attractive, young woman behind a desk greeted Cole and Derek. "Good morning, Mr. Tyler. Good morning, Mr.

Lane." She handed each of them a stack of mail and phone messages.

"Good morning, Alicia," Cole said, smiling at her.

Alicia's long, blond hair fell halfway down her back and she was as perky as a chipmunk. "There is an FBI Agent waiting for you in the lobby, Mr. Tyler. His name is Ben Walker from the San Bernardino County office."

"Now what do you suppose the FBI wants with me?" Cole looked at his phone messages. His built in radar told him this was trouble.

"He didn't seem to mind when I told him he might have to wait a little."

"I'll see him now before it gets busy, Alicia."

Cole walked into his office and shut the door. His office was surrounded with windows. He worked hard to get his name on all of those trucks and he liked to watch them come and go.

The phone rang and Alicia told him that the Agent was on his way in. Cole opened the door and a tall, slender man in a dark suit greeted him and produced a badge.

"Mr. Tyler, I'm special Agent Walker, with the FBI and I wonder if I can have a few minutes of your time? I assure you that you're not in any trouble." He smiled at Cole.

"Well, that's a relief. Please have a seat, Agent Walker. I'm making some coffee; will you have a cup with me?" Cole asked. Although he hadn't done anything wrong, it was still a relief to hear him say that.

"Yes, black please." He pulled a notepad from his jacket pocket. "I know you're a busy man, Mr. Tyler, so I'll make this as quick as I can."

Cole handed him the cup of coffee.

The Agent drank a swallow and continued with his business. "Mr. Tyler, have you ever heard of a company called Texmar that operates out of Houston, Texas?"

"Sure, they're a big name in the trucking business." Cole added creamer and stirred his coffee.

"They're in the process of expanding to a nationwide carrier. However, the FBI believes their business practices are not all legitimate. We believe they've broken laws in every state they operate in.

"They recently acquired two trucking companies on the East Coast. We think both owners of those companies were persuaded to sell against their will. Now, we believe their focus is on the West Coast. The fact is the FBI has information that your company is targeted next. If you refuse to sell, there could be problems." The Agent looked at Cole for his reaction.

"Wow, I didn't expect to hear that. What kind of people are we dealing with? Are they thugs or what?" Cole said sipping his hot coffee.

"We think they may employ their own thugs to persuade people to see things their way. We're gathering evidence on how they are acquiring these trucking companies as we speak. One owner disappeared mysteriously and the son sold immediately after. We've tried repeatedly to talk to him, but he's too scared to say anything."

"How do you know I'm on their list?" Cole asked, and sipped more of his coffee.

"I can't say how we know, but I can tell you that our information is accurate. We don't operate on a whim. We're almost certain they will approach you."

Cole looked out into the truck yard where a driver was preparing to leave on his run. He sifted through the consequences of the situation. He drank more from his coffee cup and turned back to the Agent. "What do you want me to do if they approach me?"

"All I want you to do is contact me. Act as surprised as you were when I told you. I want to record the transaction when they offer you a deal. I believe they're capable of anything and I want to put them away if they're criminals." Agent Walker took another drink from his mug.

"What if they offer me a fair price for the company?"

"That's up to you, Mr. Tyler. But no one should be forced to sell their business. It's my job to see that this company isn't bullying people. What ever you do, don't mention this meeting to anyone. If Texmar knows we're watching them, they'll never be caught. They're smart but aren't afraid to flex their muscle if they have to."

"If they pay me a visit, I'll give you a call," Cole said.

"That's all I ask." He finished his coffee.

"Agent Walker, you have my word on that." Cole stood up and shook his hand.

"Mr. Tyler, thank you for your time, and the fewer people who know about this the better."

"I assure you, no one but you and I will know anything that was said here today." Cole took the FBI Agent's card.

"By the way," the Agent said, opening the office door.

"I can't remember the last time I tasted a cup of coffee that good."

"Well, a trucker takes his coffee seriously. I'm glad you enjoyed it."

The Agent left and Cole looked out the window staring off into the long concrete yard where dozens of trucks were moving. A chill went through him as he thought about the conversation he had with the FBI Agent. He picked up the phone and told Derek that he needed to see him in his office.

A few minutes later, Derek knocked on Cole's door and sat in one of the overstuffed chairs across from his desk. "What's up?"

"Derek, does your brother still do investigation work?"

"Yeah, why?"

"I need his services as soon as possible." Cole continued to look out the window.

"What's wrong, Cole? Is Jan fooling around or something?"

"No, nothing like that. I can't say why right now."

"Sure, I'll call him right away," Derek said. "Hey, are you all right, Cole?"

"I'm fine." Cole still stared out the window with a blank look on his face.

Derek didn't pursue it any further and left.

A few minutes later, Cole picked up the call from Derek's brother.

"Garrett, Cole Tyler."

"Mr. Tyler, Derek said you need my services."

"Yes, I'm curious about a company that operates in Texas. Would that be a problem for you?"

"No problem at all. What can I do for you?"

"I'm looking for information on a company called Texmar. They operate out of Houston, Texas. I need as much information as you can dig up on them."

"Okay, I'll start right away," Garrett said.

"Just be discrete about it. Only you and I should know about this. I don't even want Derek to know."

"Absolutely, that's my business."

"Thanks, Garrett. I'd appreciate your immediate attention to this matter."

"I'll let you know something as soon as I can."

Cole hung up the phone and sorted through his phone messages. Every nerve in his body stood on end when he saw one message from Texmar in Houston Texas.

3

THE WENTWORTH FAMILY home was called The Southern Star Ranch and was located in the prime ranch country just outside of Houston, Texas. Long white fences bordered the ranch and stretched for miles. Wildflowers blanketed the pastures and meadows were dotted with tall pine and oak trees. Cattle and horses grazed the enormous interior ranges that spread for fifteen thousand acres.

Katherine Wentworth walked to the main barn of the Southern Star where a tall, slender ranch hand brushed a beautiful dark brown horse. She smiled when she took the reins from him.

"Mornin', Miss Wentworth," he said. "Beautiful day for a ride."

"Yes indeed it is." She patted the horse on the neck. Has Wendy showed up yet, Tommy?"

"Yes ma'am. She rode out about fifteen minutes ago into the northwest pasture." He motioned in the direction.

"Guess I'll have to catch up with her then." She quickly mounted the horse and kicked it into a full run right away.

The wind was loud as it passed by her ears while the horse ran as fast as he could. God, how she loved the freedom of running a horse flat out. She went to a completely different place in her mind when she was riding. There was no place on earth she would rather be than at the Southern Star Ranch.

A couple of minutes later, she saw her best friend, Wendy, in the distance waving her arms. Katherine slowed the horse to a gallop, then a fast walk, until she came within a few yards of Wendy.

Wendy Taggert lived at the next ranch over. Modest in size by the Southern Star, the ranch spread over seventeen hundred acres.

"Hey, girl," Wendy said. "You trying to set a new land speed record?"

"I'm a little late so I thought I'd make up some time." Katherine got down from the horse and tied him to a tree.

"So, what's this big secret you have to tell me?" Wendy sounded impatient.

"Just cut right to the chase huh?"

"You know me. I love this kind of stuff."

"Well, Jake and I are getting serious."

"Really, tell me more." Wendy's eyes got big.

"I think he is going to ask me to marry him."

Wendy's mouth was wide open. "No. Are you sure this is Katherine Wentworth talking? The woman who told me she would never get married again?"

"Can't a girl change her mind?" Katherine laughed.

Wendy hugged her. "Are you kidding? I'm so happy for you. So tell me all about it and don't leave any of the juicy stuff out."

The two of them talked for an hour about Katherine and Jake.

"Isn't Jake working on your father's new project on the coast?" Wendy asked.

"Yes and he loves it. His construction company is doing very well now and daddy likes him. But I'm not thrilled about him working with my father." Katherine looked out into the meadow and picked a wildflower and twirled it.

Wendy stilled smiled form ear to ear, "I'm so happy for you. I knew you would find the right guy for you one day."

"I have something else I want your opinion on." Katherine changed her tone of voice. "You remember that little private island I have in the gulf. My Grandmother left it to me in her will. I have an idea that I've been looking into lately."

"We went there once in high school remember?" Wendy laughed at the memory. "There wasn't much there as I can remember. You're not thinking of living in that old house are you?"

"I'm thinking of something much bigger than that." Katherine smiled at her friend. "I want to build a hotel there and I'm really excited about it."

Silence surrounded the two women.

"Well, am I crazy or what?" Katherine asked.

"What about your job at Texmar?"

Katherine blew out a breath of air. "Daddy is training Marty to run the company. I'm not going anywhere at Texmar."

"Why can't he see that you're ten times smarter than Marty when it comes to business?"

"It doesn't matter to him. He thinks I should have lots of babies and stay at home. Changing my father's mind is nearly impossible. I can either whine about the rest of my life or do something about it. I have to break away from Texmar and start my own business."

"What will Jake say when you tell him about this?"

"He'll think I'm nuts like you do. Then he'll do his best to talk me out of it."

"Do you want to chance that with him?"

"Wendy, I have to do what I think is best for me. I don't care what anyone else wants me to do. I'm going to do this because I know it will work."

"It sounds like a huge project. Do you know what you're getting yourself into?"

"You know me, I never know exactly what I'm getting into. But don't you see, that's what makes it so exciting."

"Just do me a favor and don't screw up your relationship with Jake. He's one man you don't want to let get away. Okay?" Wendy had a tear in her eye.

"Don't worry about me. I'll be better off away from Texmar. And if Jake won't support me, then he isn't the right guy for me."

The two girls hugged each other like sisters. They untied their horses and talked a few minutes longer.

Katherine looked at Wendy and said, "Race ya' back!"

They both jumped on their horses and brought them to a full run in seconds. The ground rumbled with the sound of two running horses. Dust slowly settled back to the ground as they got further away. Then, they were completely out of sight.

In the distance, a man was hidden in a patch of trees. He turned off the camera and the recorder with the long-range microphone.

4

A HUNDRED MILES east of Cole Tyler's trucking company, was a desert community with hundreds of golf courses and second homes to many people in Southern California.

Cole's second home sat on a golf course and had a spectacular view of the San Jacinto Mountains from every room. The desert breezes cleaned the air and brought in warm temperatures. It was like another world out there.

But today wasn't one of those carefree days for relaxing or unwinding. Garrett called him earlier and said they needed to meet somewhere in private.

Cole was drinking a glass of bourbon when the doorbell rang. He looked out his large window by his front door and saw Garrett and another younger man with him. He opened the door and greeted them. "Hello, Garrett."

"Cole it's good to see you again. I'd like you to meet Kyle Chambers. Kyle is in charge of the Texmar investigation. Kyle, Cole Tyler, owner of Tyler Transport."

The two men shook hands.

"Kyle, it's a pleasure to meet you. Come on in and have a seat in the study." Cole motioned to the large room with several bookcases surrounding it.

The two men sat on a leather couch and each took Cole's offer of a glass of bourbon.

Cole gave them the drinks and sat at his desk across from them. "So Garrett, what did you find out about Texmar?"

"We found some strange things during our investigation. We don't know quite what to make of some of them. Kyle actually did the digging so I'll let him tell you what he found," Garrett said.

Kyle took out a notepad and put it on the table in front of him. "Mr. Tyler, I first want to say, I've been in the investigation field for fifteen years. I've worked on hundreds of cases. When Garrett contacted me, and told me what to investigate, I thought it would be another routine corporate case. However, what I found in a short amount of time will probably amaze you."

Kyle took a drink of his bourbon and Cole listened without comment.

"It would be safe to say that everything about Texmar, and the man who runs it, is anything but normal. The same goes for the whole Wentworth family.

"Martin Wentworth Sr. has been married to Amanda Wentworth for thirty-two years. His wife is heavily involved in the Texas social scene. She probably has no idea what Martin does at work and probably doesn't care. She loves to raise money at events she puts on for her favorite charities.

"They have four children. Justin, the oldest boy, is not living with the family and we can't even locate him right now. However, with some time he can be found.

"Katherine, his oldest daughter, is a vice president at Texmar along with twenty-three other vice presidents of the company. She is very ambitious but daddy keeps her on a short leash.

"Marty, or Martin Jr., has a problem with drugs and likes wild women. Not the brightest mind to be in the position he is in at the company either. It gives new meaning to family and business not mixing.

"Tiffany, is his youngest daughter, and is not involved in the company. She is still in high school and the boys stand in line for her. She spends most of her time spending her father's money, which she is very good at.

"Matthew Wentworth is Martin's older brother. He is General Manager of Texmar and in charge of maintaining the trucking fleet. This guy knows his trucks and is Martin's right hand man. He is in on all of the big decisions of the company."

"On the surface, Texmar appears legitimate. However, if you look at the assets of the company, something doesn't add up. Martin Wentworth reports to the IRS that his salary is four and a half million dollars a year. His stock in Texmar pays him dividends of two million. He receives another million and change in bonuses. That's seven and a half million dollars a year. Not a bad salary for a Texas boy who never went to college."

"His ranch is worth about fifty million dollars on today's market. He owns it free and clear along with his forty-story office building and twelve regional truck terminals throughout the United States. He has about fifteen hundred trucks on the road and not one of them is over two years old. Bottom line is Martin Wentworth spends more money than he makes. Without getting into detail, he should come up about twenty million short of even breaking a profit every year." Kyle drank another swig of bourbon.

"I knew he had to have something else funding his company, so I dug a little further. It took some time but I found an offshore account with ten million dollars."

Cole looked at the San Jacinto Mountains from his window. "Looks like he's hiding some money."

Kyle looked at Garrett and back at Cole. "If that was all I found believe me, we wouldn't be having this conversation. I dug further and located two other accounts that he has hidden very well. One has twenty three million and another has a hundred and forty million."

Cole sipped his drink and turned toward the two men. "Why do you suppose he is hiding all that money?"

Garrett responded. "We didn't know how far you wanted us to go with this, Cole. The more we dig, the more we find."

Kyle took another drink and sat further back on the couch. "At this point, Mr. Tyler, we don't know how he got the money. I always check offshore accounts, but rarely find anything that size. With further investigation I can probably find a lot more."

"Tell me something, Kyle, why doesn't the IRS have this information? I mean, can't they put this guy away forever for doing this?" Cole asked.

"Martin Wentworth has a lot of power with that kind of money. More than likely, he buys politicians. He makes the money illegally then gives big contributions to their campaigns. They don't ask where his money comes from and tell the IRS to back off. Its called big business in America, Mr. Tyler," Kyle said.

Cole took a drink of bourbon. "Not exactly a model citizen is he?"

"That's as far as we went, Cole," Garrett said.

Kyle finished his drink and put the glass on a table. "We found a lot of information in a short amount of time. How far we go from here is up to you."

Cole weighed his options. "How safe is it investigating this guy, Kyle?"

"He'll kill me if he finds out what I'm doing. This business isn't safe and I don't pretend it is."

"How can you be sure that he isn't listening to us right now?" Cole asked.

Kyle took a small, thin, black box out of his jacket and sat it on Cole's desk. "That's how I know. This box emits electronic signals that block any bugs or long range microphones. I'd like you to keep this one here and take one to your office. Let me warn you, Martin Wentworth utilizes the same type of technology at Texmar. He is extremely careful about information leaking out."

Cole stood up from behind his desk. "Kyle, I'm impressed with your work and I want you to continue. I need to know more about Texmar and the Wentworth's. I think this guy wants my company and I want to know what makes him tick."

Kyle looked at him with a concerned look. "I was hoping you would say that. But let me warn you, this guy plays hardball and I would be careful.

"I haven't met the guy yet, but he sent me an invitation to a big barbecue he is having at the Southern Star Ranch," Cole said.

Kyle spoke with concern in his voice. "Just be careful, Mr. Tyler. Martin Wentworth is ruthless when he wants something. There's a possibility, no matter what we do, we won't be able to stop him."

5

AT NINE A.M. Marty was supposed to be in his father's office. He drank some more strong coffee trying to sober up before the meeting. He heard a knock on his office door and his sister, Katherine, walked in.

"Morning, little brother. Care to share a cup of coffee with a low life vice president?"

"Come on in, sis. I've been summoned to the big office first thing this morning. Sorry, I'm already late."

"Well, I guess I can't keep you then. We both know how daddy hates to be kept waiting. Can I steal you away for lunch today?" She straightened his tie.

"Sure, lunch at the club, say twelve thirty?" Marty put his suit jacket on.

"That's a date. I want to bend your ear about something."

Marty rolled his eyes. "Not you too. I'm getting hit from all sides today."

"Hard times at the top of the ladder?"

"It's just, you know how pop can nag about things if their not done the way he would do it."

"Marty, you're going to have to stand your ground with him. He'll respect you more for it."

"We'll talk more at lunch. I'm already late."

"Give em' hell, kid."

Marty smiled back at her walking down the long hallway towards his father's office. He flew by Martin's secretary into his father's office.

His Uncle, Matthew, sat in one of the leather chairs.

His father greeted him. "Well, glad you can squeeze us into your busy schedule. We've got a lot to cover so lets get started."

Marty poured himself more coffee, sat down in a chair, and gritted his teeth for another session with his uncle and father. He squinted his eyes from the bright light the floor to ceiling windows brought into the room.

Martin sat behind his desk and frowned at Marty. "First of all, the drugs stop immediately. Don't try and tell me you're not doing drugs because I know better. I'm wasting my time showing you how to run a multi billion-dollar corporation when you clutter your mind with that crap. If I find out you're taking drugs again, I'll make fertilizer out of the guy who supplies you. Got it?"

Marty frowned. "Pop, it's Viatsi's nephew. I don't think we want to mess with the Mafia."

Martin raised his voice. "Let me tell you something, Marty. I don't give a hoot in hell if the President of the United States is the one selling you this stuff. If I get wind of anyone selling you more drugs, he's dead! It interferes with my company and I won't have it!"

"Okay, point made. Just stop yelling," Marty said.

"Marty, the trick in business is not what you are but what you appear to be. If word got out that you were on drugs, what kind of image would that project for Texmar?" Martin paused and took a swig of his coffee.

"God, do we have to keep talking about this?" Marty rubbed his aching head.

"Marty, you've got to be sharp to run this outfit. I want success for this company and for you too. Drugs won't make that happen. Besides, we don't need to draw attention to us. Lord only knows, if we operated on the straight and narrow, we would have been out of business years ago."

Marty stared at the floor, listening to his father lecture him. He was trying to block the words out of his mind.

His father finally finished, turning his attention to business again. "Now, Matt, what have we got on Tyler Transport?"

Matthew handed Martin a piece of paper with information about the company. "The evaluation came in early this morning. It's worth eighteen million. His equipment is in excellent shape and it's in a prime location. We should get this company as quick as we can."

Martin's phone buzzed and his secretary told him Cole Tyler was on line one. He picked up the phone and immediately like a switch turned into another person.

"Mr. Tyler, Martin Wentworth. I know you're a busy man so I'll be brief. I want to extend you a personal invitation to my barbecue. I'll take care of all your travel plans. I'll send the company jet for you and as many people as you would like to bring. I'd also like you to stay at my ranch as my guest."

"Mr. Wentworth, I am a little curious why you even invited me. I mean, we haven't even met before." Cole said.

"Well, let's just say we have a common interest in the trucking business. I would rather talk more after I get your belly full of genuine Texas barbecue. Believe me, Mr. Tyler, I'll make it worth your while to come," Martin said.

"It just seems like a long way to come for a barbecue."

"Believe me, Mr. Tyler, in Texas we take our barbecues serious. I think you'll find it much more than throwing some meat on the grill in the back yard."

"Okay, I accept your invitation," Cole said.

"Fantastic. I'll look forward to meeting you. My secretary will fill you in on the details." Martin punched a button and hung up the phone while Matthew and Marty stared at him.

Marty spoke to his father. "What are you going to do to get this guys company?"

"Anything it takes, son. I'll wine and dine him first, and if he won't sell his company to me, then I'll take it. That company is going to be a part of Texmar soon so I want all of his accounts protected from competitors, Matt. See to it that his major accounts are in our pocket and ready to move on my notice."

Marty acted like he was interested. "Then you'll shut his accounts down if he won't sell?"

Martin smiled at him. "That's right. Power is what it's all about. You either have it or you don't. To be successful in business you need as much power as you can get. We need his company to complete our move to be a nationwide carrier. Once we have the ability to travel into any state with our trucks, our distribution network will be in place."

"Then what do we do?" Marty said.

His father and uncle looked at him shaking their heads.

"Marty, are you sure you're a Wentworth? That's a dumb question, son," Martin said.

Matthew chuckled at his nephew.

"Hey, I'm trying to learn this stuff," Marty said.

Martin smiled at his son. "Why don't you work with Dillon on Tyler's accounts? The more we know about this guy, and the way he operates, the sooner we can take over his company."

Katherine waited for Marty in the bar of their club and sipped on her second margarita. She smiled at her brother as he approached her table.

"Hey, sis. I ran a little late from the meeting. The old man was long winded today." Marty sat down and flagged the waitress down for a drink.

"Well I know how busy you've been lately and I really appreciate you coming."

"What's up? Sounds like something serious."

"It is, and I want you to keep what is said here between us. Daddy will find out soon enough on his own."

"Hey, that goes without saying. Besides, I don't want to lose your trust." He took a long drink of his double shot of whiskey as soon as the waitress set it down.

Katherine took a deep breath and proceeded to tell Marty her plans. "Well, I'm thinking of leaving the company."

"What! You can't be serious?" Marty was so loud that people turned to look at them.

"I can't believe you're so surprised. You know daddy will never let me do anything important at Texmar. He's keeping me there cooped up in the office giving me meaningless jobs."

"But leaving the company isn't the way to go, sis. I need you there with me when he hands me control of the company. I can't do it without you."

"You're gonna' have to, Marty. All I've ever done is talk to daddy about this but he doesn't budge one inch. I've spent twelve years trying to convince him to let me have more control of the company. I can't spend any more time spinning my wheels at a dead end job. I have my own ideas and I have to pursue them now."

"Wow, this is a bombshell I never expected. When do you plan on telling the old man?"

"Soon. It's time to make my move."

Marty finished his whiskey and ordered another. "What do you plan on doing?"

"The island that grandma' left me has been sitting there for years waiting for me to make something out of it. Marty, I want to build a hotel on Paradise Island and turn it into a tropical paradise."

Marty's eyes grew big and he almost lost his breath. "What? That's a terrible idea. The money it will take will be astronomical. Besides, the island is six miles out in the gulf. Who would go out there and how would they even get there?"

"Thanks for being so supportive. I haven't worked out all of the details yet, but believe me, it will be a money maker when I get through with it."

"I don't want to bust your bubble here, sis, but this sounds like a crazy idea."

"When have you ever known me not to be a little crazy? It's perfect for me."

"Well, the old man isn't going to like it one bit. I'll bet he goes ballistic when you tell him." The waitress brought him a second drink and his eyes undressed her from head to toe.

Katherine sighed. "I suppose when I offer to bring him in on the deal, he'll refuse."

"You can bet on it. You'll have trouble getting anyone to finance that kind of a deal with you."

"Do you feel the same way?"

"Sorry, sis. I don't think it's a good business decision."

Katherine looked disappointed. "Okay, I just thought you would support me on this."

"You know I love you but I really think you're about to do something stupid."

"I appreciate your honesty, but one day you'll be sorry you didn't come in on this deal with me. I need more money than I have to make the deal work. I just wanted you to have first shot at it."

Marty stood up. "I'll be right back. I'm gonna' go use the restroom." He walked to into the restroom and pulled his cell phone from his jacket. He quickly dialed numbers and put the phone up to his ear. "Pop, we've got trouble."

6

AT SEVEN P.M. Katherine arrived in a limousine at the Houston airport.

She boarded the private jet and within minutes, they were flying over the Gulf of Mexico. Katherine looked to see if she could see her tiny island. She spotted it and watched it fade away as the jet gained altitude. She closed her eyes and thought about the transformation of her island.

A few hours later when the jet approached Las Vegas, Katherine looked at the lights glowing through the darkness from many miles away. It was a spectacular sight from the air and she felt the excitement begin to grow inside her.

The jet touched down at McCarran airport and a waiting limo swiftly took her away. A short time later, she arrived at the Lucky Star Casino on the Las Vegas strip.

The lights cascaded down the front of the hotel and produced exciting visions of her own hotel. She heard people cheering from the craps and blackjack tables as she walked into the lobby.

Once she arrived at her room, she was pleased to see that Leo had given her the Marquis suite. It was the very best the hotel had to offer.

The bellman opened the drapes and Katherine immediately went to the window and looked at the spectacular view of the all of the many lights of the Las Vegas strip.

The suite had two bedrooms, two bathrooms, and an oversize living room. A big screen television occupied one corner with two sofas in the middle of the room. A dining room table and eight chairs were in another direction. Long stem, red roses placed in large vases were in every room and made the suite smell wonderful.

Three exterior balconies each had a commanding view of the strip.

The phone rang and Katherine picked it up.

"How is my little Texas tornado this evening?" Leo spoke with an Italian accent.

"Leo, everything is wonderful and I love the beautiful flowers. You're so sweet." Katherine smelled a rose.

"I would like to have a midnight supper with you tonight."

"That sounds wonderful, Leo. Can you give me a little time to get ready?"

"Of course. Just after midnight, I will send someone to escort you. I have a special place where we will dine this evening."

"See you then," Katherine said.

He was the most romantic guy she would probably ever meet in her life. She knew he would try to seduce her tonight, and she didn't have a problem with it. It was Leo's way. He loved women, married or not. He was a little dangerous and that excited her.

At two minutes before midnight, the phone rang and Katherine said she was ready. There was a knock on the door, and a tall, good-looking man in a black tuxedo offered her his arm. They proceeded down the hall to a private elevator.

When the elevator doors opened, Leo was standing in front of her. He was dressed in a dark blue Armani suit and held out a single red rose for her.

"Good evening, Miss Wentworth. You look gorgeous always." He handed her the rose and kissed her on the cheek.

"Leo, it's wonderful to see you again. I've missed you so much." Katherine hugged and kissed him.

"Please, walk with me. I have something I want you to see," Leo said, taking her arm.

They walked a few steps and looked at a breathtaking view of the Las Vegas strip on top of his casino.

Thirty-foot palm trees surrounded the roof of his hotel. Giant bird of paradise plants sat in huge pots in between the trees. Banana trees, with bunches of green bananas hanging off some of the branches, perfectly blended with the rest of the vegetation.

The scent of tropical flowers filled the air with an exotic aroma.

Several waterfalls spilled into pools and sounded as soothing as soft music.

A perfectly placed table sat waiting for them.

"Do you approve of my little get away spot?"

"Yes, it's like paradise here." Katherine smiled at him.

"Well, I have to leave the action once in awhile. This place gives me the peace that I seek."

Katherine and Leo dined by one of the waterfalls and enjoyed the view from their own piece of paradise. They hadn't seen each other for awhile and caught up on the lost time. Katherine loved to talk to Leo. He was easy to like and very good looking. But when the opportunity came for business, she didn't waste time getting to the point.

"Leo, what would you say if I wanted to build my own hotel and casino?"

He paused without saying anything for a minute and his mood changed quickly. "You can't be serious?"

"Why yes, I'm quite serious." Her Southern accent was slight but still noticeable.

"It's a very tricky business and you can lose a fortune unless you know what you're doing."

Katherine frowned. "Leo, I thought you would be happy about this. You're the first person I've approached about this project."

Leo lit a cigar, stood up, walked to the edge of the roof, and looked over. "Are you sure you want to get mixed up in this crazy business?"

Katherine followed him putting her arm on his. "Yes I'm sure."

"Look out at the casinos and tell me what you see."

Katherine looked at several casinos on the strip. "I see money. I see lots of money being made in beautiful buildings.

Leo puffed on his cigar and paused for a moment. "You only see what is on the surface, not the way it really is. There is a dark side to all of this, Katherine. You may not want to get involved."

"Have you ever known me to take on anything easy?"

"It's risky. Are you sure you can pull it off and still make a profit? I mean, you don't know anything about the business."

"I have a good teacher," she said, smiling at him.

"I don't know if I can teach you everything."

Katherine put her hand on his cheek. "Hey, remember me, the one who got you into the deal of a lifetime not that long ago? This deal is bigger than that, and I'm bringing it to you first."

"I would be cautious about getting into the hotel and casino business. Why don't you stick to real estate? We both know you are good at that."

Katherine took a drink of her wine. She watched the people walking down on the sidewalk. They were very small from this height. "Leo, tell me something and please be honest. Has my father warned you to stay out of this deal?"

He was silent for a moment and looked nervous about her question. "What makes you ask that?" He looked away from her and puffed on his cigar.

Katherine studied his eyes before she answered. "I adore you, and I trust you, but I can't waste time with this if my father threw a wrench into this deal. Just be honest and tell me if he had anything to do with you not wanting in this deal with me."

Leo seemed uncomfortable about her question. "He could easily put me out of business, Katherine. He is very powerful and I don't want to lose my casino." He couldn't look at her.

Katherine put her hand on his shoulder and kissed him on the cheek. "Thanks for being honest and I want you to know I don't blame you. This is my problem and I'll take care of it."

Katherine walked away and the man that escorted her up opened the elevator door for her.

"Would you like an escort, Miss Wentworth?" He offered her his arm.

"No thanks, I need to be alone now."

Leo walked over to a man who stood in the shadows. "Tell Mr. Wentworth I fulfilled my obligation."

7

MARTY'S PHONE RANG at eight minutes after three in the morning. His head was still spinning from all the drinks he had at the club with Katherine. He didn't remember driving home or even how he got in his bed. The phone sounded like a freight train that wouldn't go away. He answered it so the ringing would stop.

His father's voice roared through his ear. "Marty, we have to take care of some urgent business. Get down to my office right away."

He glanced at his digital clock. “Pop, do you know what time it is?”

“I’m not going to tell you twice, now get your butt down there! Use the private elevator in the back.”

The phone went dead and Marty reluctantly got up.

When he arrived at Texmar, he took the hidden elevator that was only used by Martin, Matthew, and himself. A locked door secluded it. He put his card in the private slot, and his mind questioned why he was there.

By the time his curiosity caught up with him, he was walking into Martin’s office. Standing in front of him was his father, Uncle Matthew and another man he didn’t recognize.

Martin spoke to him as soon as he shut the door. “Don’t you look like hell? Marty, this is Austin. He helps us when we need special work done for us.”

The man shook hands with Marty and nodded his head.

Marty was still trying to focus his eyes from only two hours of sleep and a lot of alcohol.

Martin eyed everyone. “The helicopter will be here shortly. Let’s get up to the roof and meet it.”

The three men walked ahead of Marty and seemed to know where they were going. Marty followed them like a lost puppy. He was glad to be on their side because they looked like they were going into battle.

As soon as they got to the roof, the helicopter landed. They all boarded and took off immediately.

Everything moved so quick that Marty thought all of this could be a dream. Seeing Houston from the air in early morning was a welcome relief for his tired eyes.

The ride lasted ten minutes and the helicopter sat down in an empty field, just out of town.

Everyone got out, stood in the large field, and seemed to be waiting for something to happen.

A semi truck and trailer pulled off the road and came towards them. It stopped, shut off the lights, and the driver left the motor running. The driver got out and rolled down the landing gear to the trailer. He pulled the release for the fifth wheel trailer. Then, he took the airlines away from the trailer.

Austin walked around to the passenger side of the truck and pulled a man out of the seat. His hands were tied and he was gagged. Austin brought him around to the front of the truck where everyone was standing.

Marty gasped when he looked at his face.

Martin looked at his son's reaction. "So you recognize this punk?"

"Pop I...."

"Save it." Martin interrupted.

"But Viatsi will kill you for this. It's his nephew. Don't you realize who the Viatsi crime family is?"

"I'm shakin' in my boots. I warned you about buying drugs again, didn't I? Remember when I said that I would kill the dealer who sold you drugs? I'm a man of my word, Marty, and I'm about to prove that to you."

"Yeah but this is crazy. It's just drugs."

"Just drugs? Let me educate you real quick. I won't have drugs destroy you or my company. When I told you not to buy any more drugs, it was a warning! We warned him too! But you did it anyway, and in my book, that tells me you don't think I mean business. Hook him up, Austin." Martin pointed to the semi.

Austin tied the man's legs to the front of the trailer. Then, he tied his hands to the tractor.

The driver got into the tractor and put it in low gear.

Viatsi couldn't say anything because of the gag in his mouth. But he screamed through the gag and the horrified look on his face communicated his horror.

Austin whispered something in Martin's ear and Martin nodded.

Marty turned to his father. "Why do I have to watch this?"

"So the next time I warn you about something you'll know I mean business. I don't like this either, but sometimes it's necessary. Make a wish, Austin."

Austin nodded to the truck driver and the truck took off.

It was over in two seconds and was the bloodiest thing Marty had ever seen. It sounded like scissors cutting through paper when the flesh tore. Blood was all over everything.

He closed his eyes in disbelief after it happened. The memory of it would be etched in his mind forever.

Martin stared at Marty. "I'll kill a hundred people the same way if I have to." He walked toward the helicopter.

Matthew put his hand on his nephew's shoulder. "If I were you, kid, I'd get straight in a hurry."

Marty staggered back to the helicopter. He didn't remember much about the flight back to Texmar, but it seemed like they were back instantly. He followed his father and uncle into the building, but Austin disappeared. If this was a dream, he was ready to wake up.

The three men reached Martin's office, and Matthew made drinks at the bar.

Marty downed the first drink and quickly got another. He felt like he could drink the whole bottle.

Martin saw the still horrified look on Marty's face. "This is not a game were playing. If I have a problem, I eliminate it. That's what we did tonight."

Marty glared at his father. "You mutilated that guy. Why kill him like that?"

"Because it sends a message. You don't mess with us or we'll tear you to pieces. Only the strong survive and that's the only reason we're still here. You'll learn that when you have power, you rarely have to use it. People know what you're capable of."

"Okay, I messed up by buying more drugs and I'm sorry. I give you my word I won't do it again."

"What you saw tonight remains between us, and no one else. That includes your sister. If I'm going to show you the business, then you better learn how things work. Now go home and get cleaned up."

Marty quickly finished his drink got up and left the office without comment.

Matthew looked at his brother. "God, Martin. That was the bloodiest thing I've ever seen."

Martin took a drink. "It's exactly what Marty needed. I guarantee he'll never be the same again."

8

ON FRIDAY MORNING, the Black limousine pulled up to the private hangers at Ontario airport. Texmar's corporate jet was waiting with the engines running. The limo driver quickly opened the doors and Cole, Jan, Derek, and Crystal boarded the jet. The driver loaded the bags in the cargo hold, and the jet taxied to the runway.

After take off the pilot informed them, the flight time to Houston, Texas was two hours.

The trip didn't seem to take that long, although Cole's watch confirmed it did. The humidity was the first thing everyone noticed, when they stepped off the jet at the Houston airport. It was much higher than California and made the ninety-degree heat seem even hotter.

Another limousine waited on the runway to take them to the Southern Star Ranch. After a twenty-minute ride, they saw the long white fences bordering the ranch.

The driver spoke with a strong Texas drawl. "Folks on the left, is the starting point of the Southern Star Ranch."

All four of them looked out the windows with curiosity.

"The ranch is just over fifteen thousand acres, and I think you'll agree, it's one of the most beautiful spots on the planet. It is totally self sufficient with its own power station and water supply.

"The Wentworth's purchased the ranch in 1962, and have since added to its size, by purchasing several smaller ranches that once surrounded it.

"Over ten thousand cattle and fifteen hundred horses roam the interior ranges. Directly behind the ranch is a ten thousand-acre wildlife preserve.

"Several guest homes are placed throughout the ranch, which is where you will be staying while you are here. The Wentworth home is located one mile to the West of here.

"Please enjoy your stay and welcome to the Southern Star Ranch," the driver said, pulling up to the guesthouse.

It was a beautiful two level home decorated in Western style. That didn't surprise anyone; after all, they were in Texas. The house was surprisingly warm and homey.

Jan unpacked and Cole answered the phone when it rang two times.

Martin Wentworth welcomed his guests. "Mr. Tyler? How was your flight?"

"Very nice, thank you," Cole said.

"My pleasure. Listen, I want you to enjoy the ranch today and unwind from your trip. I think you'll find our little spread here to your liking. Tomorrow at eleven a.m., I'll send a car for your party to come to the main house to meet my wife and family. The barbecue will start at one o'clock. Sound all right to you?"

"Yes, that sounds fine."

"All right then. If you need anything just pick up the phone and Dean will assist you. He is assigned to you for anything you need."

"Thank you, Mr. Wentworth. I'll be looking forward to meeting you and your family tomorrow." Cole hung up the phone and told everyone what Martin said.

Derek and Crystal decided to go on a horseback ride.

Jan was more of a city girl and wanted to explore the ranch by car.

Cole was pleased to see a Jeep parked in the garage. He took the top down and drove Jan into the pastures of the magnificent ranch. When he spotted a meadow covered with wildflowers, they both got out and absorbed the moment.

"Seems like paradise doesn't it?" Cole said to Jan.

A dozen horses grazed in the pasture to their left. Their tails swished as they constantly ate grass.

"Yes and the wildflowers are so beautiful," she said, picking a flower and smelling it.

Cole looked at the enormous size of the ranch. It was the most breathtaking and peaceful place he had ever seen.

In the distance, he saw a rider on a horse heading towards them. The horse trotted at a slow pace and as the horse got closer he could tell the rider was a woman.

She slowed the horse to a walk and then stopped to greet them. "Howdy, folks, I'm Wendy. I hope you don't mind me intruding on your privacy. I'm supposed to meet someone here but she hasn't shown up yet. Mind if I wait for a few minutes?"

"We don't mind at all. I'm Cole and this is Jan."

Wendy climbed off of the horse, tied it to a tree, and took her riding gloves off. "Pleased to meet ya'. Where are you folks from?"

"We're from Southern California. We just came out for the weekend," Cole said.

"Well, the Wentworth's are putting on one of their famous barbecues tomorrow. If you like country music, Trevor Jackson is gonna' be playing there."

Jan's eyes grew big. "Really? Trevor Jackson is really going to be here tomorrow?"

Wendy smiled at her. "Sure is and he's as cute as a bug's butt too. I got to meet him yesterday at the Wentworth's. Mr. Wentworth owns the studio that records his music. He loves coming to the Southern Star Ranch. Katherine kinda' had a fling with him about a year ago. That's who I'm waiting for and I think I see her coming."

Everyone squinted, as Katherine came in with the sun to her back.

When she got close enough to see, Cole looked at her and felt something he had never felt in his entire life. He couldn't explain exactly what it was, but he couldn't take his eyes off of Katherine. It was her look, her actions, and her smile. It was everything about her.

She climbed down from the horse, and when her ice blue eyes met Cole's, he felt like she had the same feeling. She stood close to him violating the invisible margin of space strangers usually keep. She held her hand out and every nerve in Cole's body stood on end when they touched.

Jan and Wendy both looked shocked.

Katherine broke the silence. "I'm Katherine Wentworth. You must be Cole Tyler?"

He had to bring his mind back to earth. She wasn't just another pretty face. She was drop-dead gorgeous. "Have we met before?"

"No, but I make it my business to know who's coming to the ranch. So, Mr. Tyler, will you be attending our little barbecue tomorrow?"

"Yes, your father invited me."

Jan frowned at the way Cole was looking at her.

Katherine mounted her horse and Wendy followed. "I hope you folks will forgive me but I must go for my ride now. Mr. Tyler, pleasure meeting you, and I hope to see you tomorrow. Who knows, maybe I can steal you away for a horseback ride and show you the real Southern Star Ranch." Katherine kicked her horse and disappeared over the hill as fast as she came. Wendy followed close behind her.

Jan approached Cole. "Steal you away for a ride. What a bitch! And you, staring at her like she's some sort of goddess or something."

Cole had to bring himself back from his experience. "Give it a rest, Jan. I'm not going to listen to you moan and groan about it."

"Well it's obvious you don't care what I think. She might have a lot of money but she's not going to humiliate me." Jan walked away.

Cole stared in Katherine's direction. "What the hell just happened?"

9

AT FIVE TWENTY in the morning, Cole carried his steaming cup of coffee onto the front porch of the guesthouse. He leaned over the rail and waited for the sunrise to light up the Southern Star Ranch.

The first traces of the pink dawn were just starting to nudge at the edges of the horizon. The sun lit the surrounding hills and endless meadows covered with Texas Bluebonnets and Paintbrush wildflowers. One hundred-foot tall cottonwood trees dotted the pastures and very old oaks dropped thousands of acorns on the ground.

He smelled the dew from the pasture as the sun slowly warmed it. Steam rose from the ground and filled the air as it evaporated and mixed with the smell of range grass. He filled his lungs with the morning air mixed with the aroma of his fresh brewed coffee and savored this special moment.

The mockingbirds sang their morning songs to remind the world another day was starting. Doves cooed and pecked the ground looking for food. Monarch butterflies fluttered gracefully over the grass.

The sun slowly changed the sky to a lighter blue as it rose higher over the mountain range exposing more of the beautiful ranch hidden by the darkness of night.

Texas longhorn cattle grazed in the distant pastures below the hills before they met the mountains. In another direction, chocolate colored horses ate grass. Their beautiful coats shined when the sun hit them.

A rooster crowed in the distance and Cole smiled taking in every second from this completely different world than what he was used to. A cool breeze brushed against his face and the wind filled his ears for a moment. He felt a tingling sensation on the back of his neck and his cheeks flushed red with color.

Cole sipped his coffee and let the magic of the sunrise engulf him. Although this was his first time to the Southern Star Ranch, he felt like he belonged here.

His thoughts suddenly shifted to a shadow coming toward him. Before he could tell what it was, a woman's voice surprised him.

"Mornin', cowboy. Up a little early aren't you?" She dismounted from her horse.

Cole recognized Katherine's voice before the darkness allowed him to see her. The sunrise was a spectacular way to start the day. But when Katherine showed up, it made it perfect. "Well, good morning to you too, Miss Wentworth."

"Everyone calls me Katherine."

"Everyone calls me Cole," he said, not being able to hold back a big smile. "Coffee?"

"No thanks." She tied her horse to the porch railing.

"I could say we've got to stop meeting like this, but I wouldn't mean it. Do you always go riding at five thirty in the morning?"

"Do you get up to watch the sunrise every morning?"

Cole liked her sassy attitude. It made her so genuine. He looked out again at the ranch. "The sunrise here is like a religious experience. It's as if heaven opened its gates and let all of its beauty escape on one place on the earth."

"You really mean that, don't you?" Katherine stood next to him taking off her leather riding gloves.

"Yes I do. You're so lucky to live here."

"How would you like to see something else that's incredibly beautiful? That is, if you can keep a secret."

"What, some secret part of the ranch?"

Katherine smiled at him. "Trust me; it will be an experience you won't soon forget."

"Has anyone ever told you it's hard to say no to you?"

"So does that mean you'll come?"

Cole looked back at the guesthouse, then at Katherine. "Let's go."

Katherine reached for her cell phone, dialed some numbers, and talked for about a minute. "Hop on." She untied her horse and climbed into her saddle.

She helped Cole on the back of the horse and they rode away. They rode until they reached a clearing a mile away.

"We'll wait here a few minutes for our ride," she said, jumping down and tying her horse to a tree.

Cole and Katherine talked for a few minutes until they heard a helicopter approach.

"What's going on?" He looked at the helicopter descending down to them.

"That's our ride."

The helicopter came down quickly and landed in the clearing. The wind from the moving blades was intense.

Katherine grabbed Cole's hand and they ran with their heads ducked low. They entered the side door and closed it. The helicopter lifted off the ground.

Katherine put a headset on and motioned to Cole to put one on too.

"Where in the world are you taking me?" Cole talked into the microphone.

"Just a short ride off the coast."

"Which coast?"

"The coast of Texas, silly. I promise to have you back before breakfast. Okay?"

"I'm not about to say no to you now."

The helicopter offered a commanding view of the ranch. As it headed further out, the Texas coastline came into view. The rising sun glared orange off the water in the Gulf of Mexico. The sky was getting lighter blue by the minute. The pilot made a quick descent and landed on a small island a few miles from land.

Cole and Katherine got out and crouched under the rotor blades. The sandy soil made it hard to walk. When they were a hundred yards away, they heard the helicopter motor wind down.

"So, what do you think of my little island?" She watched Cole's eyes widen.

"Your island? Why doesn't that surprise me?"

"My grandmother owned it since the nineteen twenties. She died twelve years ago and left it to me."

"Wow, what a great place." Cole looked it over. "How big is it?"

"A mile and a half long and a half mile wide at its widest point."

Cole felt the warm breeze blow in from the Gulf of Mexico and let his imagination run wild. Although the island was almost bare, he envisioned many scenarios of what it could be. "Do you plan to build a house here and have your own tropical paradise?"

"You forget you're in Texas now. We tend to think a little bigger. I want to build a hotel."

"Yes, with all oceanfront rooms and swimming pools with waterfalls. What a great idea."

Cole's attitude spoke volumes to her. "Do you mean that? You think it's a good idea?"

"I think it's a fantastic idea."

"It's just... well; you're the first person that doesn't think I'm crazy for wanting to build a hotel here."

"What kind of money would it take?"

"A couple hundred million to build it right," she said.

"Wow! You're right, you do things big here."

"This place will be a gold mine once it's finished."

"Building a hotel on your own tropical island. I envy you, Katherine."

Cole turned toward her and she kissed him on the lips. He didn't want it to ever stop. The kiss surprised him and he was completely lost in the moment.

She looked deep in his eyes. "Thanks for believing in my dream."

"You know, if circumstances were different."

"I feel the same way and I just met you. But I better get you back and keep my promise." She broke the embrace and walked toward the helicopter with Cole by her side. They boarded and were back in the air within a minute.

"Once around the block, Jimmy." Katherine instructed her pilot.

"Yes ma'am," he said.

Katherine pointed down. "There's one narrow spot on the tip of the island where we will have to bring up sand from the ocean floor to fill in."

"Looks like you have company," Cole said, pointing to a large yacht in the water anchored off the Southern tip of the island.

Katherine picked up a pair of binoculars and studied the boat carefully. "Well, we know he's got class by the size of the yacht. What he doesn't have is permission to dock." She wrote down some information on a note pad.

The flight back to the ranch took only minutes. The helicopter dropped them off and disappeared with the hum from its distant motor fading away.

Katherine and Cole rode double on the horse until they were a hundred yards from the guesthouse.

"I hope I didn't get you into too much trouble with your girlfriend," she said.

Cole jumped off of the back of the horse. "Let me worry about that. Thanks for showing me your island."

"Can we keep the hotel idea just between us for now? I don't want a lot of people to know just yet."

"Absolutely, just between friends."

"Thanks for believing in me, Cole."

"I want to see your hotel a reality someday."

"I promise you'll stay in my hotel one day. And I always keep my promises." She kicked her horse and rode away.

He watched her until she was gone. He found himself reluctant to leave her, and he knew she felt the same way.

10

MARTIN WAS UP early taking care of business that couldn't wait. In his office, at the ranch, he spoke into the phone. "Austin, if the man refuses to sell then cut his damn throat. I don't have the time to wait." He drank coffee from his large cup.

Austin responded. "I don't think the man knows we mean business, Mr. Wentworth. I wanted you to make the call before I did anything with this guy."

"Call me when it's done so I can make a move. It's the last link I need on the East Coast and it's an important one."

"Consider it done, sir."

"Appreciate it, Austin. I'll talk to you soon." Martin hung up the phone.

When Cole and his guests arrived at the main ranch house, it was twenty minutes after eleven.

Workers were setting up hundreds tables and dozens of tents on a grass area the size of a football field.

Indians dressed in buckskin outfits and colorful headdresses practiced their tribal dances.

A truck unloaded bulls into a rodeo arena that seated a thousand people.

Chefs prepared food on enormous grills. In another direction, a stage was being prepared for Trevor Jackson, who would play all of his country music hits for the crowd.

The Wentworth home was a large ranch style house surrounded by dark green lawns. Rows of multi-colored flowers filled the air with a sweet aroma. Perfectly groomed hedges lined the walkway up to the house.

An older man, dressed as a butler, opened the door and welcomed them.

Martin Wentworth immediately entered the oversize room and introduced everyone. "I would like to welcome all of you to the Southern Star Ranch. I'm Martin Wentworth;

this is my wife, Amanda, and our youngest daughter, Tiffany."

They both smiled and said hello to them.

"I would like to introduce Katherine, our oldest daughter, and her fiancé, Jake Bolton."

Cole's face flushed and his heart sank a little when he heard that. He noticed Katherine smiling at him. Her fiancé was tall and good-looking enough to warrant a second look from most women. For some strange reason, he felt a little jealous. Katherine finally looked his way again and it perked him right up.

"I apologize for my youngest son, Marty, not being here. He had urgent business that required his immediate attention."

Cole watched Katherine roll her eyes. He pointed to everyone as he introduced them. "I'm Cole Tyler. This is Jan Moore, and Derek and Crystal Lane. It's a pleasure to meet all of you.

Martin looked at Jan and Crystal. "I understand you two ladies are fans of Trevor Jackson."

Both of them opened their mouths wide.

Jan spoke up. "Yes, we both love his songs."

Martin pointed to double doors down the hallway. "If you open the doors to the library, you'll find him waiting to talk to you."

Jan and Crystal squealed like a couple of high school girls. Derek went along to see what the fuss was about.

Martin smiled at their anticipation, and then looked at Cole. "You think we could talk for a few minutes in my office?"

"Absolutely." It didn't surprise Cole that he was eager to do business. In fact, he fully expected it. He followed Martin to a different part of the house and entered the office.

The large room was as big as some people's homes. A pool table sat to one side of the room and custom-made pool cues in glass racks hung on the walls. The walls also displayed actual pistols from the Alamo, framed in thick oak cases. The room had several leather chairs, two couches, and a full size bar.

Martin's desk was a conversation piece in itself. "Sam Houston had this very desk in his office a hundred years ago," Martin explained.

But the gigantic flag of Texas was the focal point of the whole room. It was spread out on the wall behind Martin's desk and measured twenty feet wide and was almost as tall. Spotlights recessed in the ceiling pointed towards it from six different angles.

Cole thought if anyone could win an award for first impressions, Martin Wentworth would win hands down.

"Have a seat, Mr. Tyler. I hope you don't mind me taking you away from your friends for a few minutes. Can I offer you a drink? I have a special whiskey blended for me I think you'll enjoy."

Cole sat in an over stuffed, leather chair close to the historic desk. "I'd love to try it. He took the drink and sipped it. "That is good whiskey. So, what can I do for you, Mr. Wentworth?"

"Well, Mr. Tyler, it's what I can do for you. I believe in getting right down to business, so I'll get to the point. As you probably know, I'm expanding my operation and I'm looking to the West Coast as part of my expansion."

Cole looked around the room and felt his face flush. "Okay, how do I fit in to this?"

"Mr. Tyler, I want to buy you out."

Cole swallowed more of the whiskey before he responded. "My business is not for sale. I spent twenty years of my life building that company."

"I realize that and I'm willing to compensate you well for building such a fine company. See, Mr. Tyler, if I start up my own company out there it costs me a lot more than if I take over an existing one. So I'm willing to pass on some of that savings to you in the purchase price."

Cole appeared calm on the outside, but inside it was a different story. "So, what kind of a price did you have in mind?"

"I like a man that puts his cards on the table." Martin smiled at him. "I'll be honest and tell you that I've evaluated your company and three others in your area. How does eighty million sound?" Martin looked for his reaction.

"So that's what you're offering me?"

Martin maintained eye contact. "I said I would compensate you for taking over your business. I'll give you another million in cash under the table. That's tax-free money, Mr. Tyler. You can put that money in your pocket and no one but you and me has to know about it."

"Well, Mr. Wentworth, that's an interesting offer. You do realize that I was totally unprepared for this and I'll need some time to think it over."

"Oh absolutely. I don't expect a man to make a decision like that on a whim. I want you to think about it and get back with me as soon as you can. In the meantime, get your belly full on some of that Texas barbecue out there. And you think about how you're going to spend all that money." Martin grinned at him.

Cole stood up without expression.

"Oh, one more thing, Mr. Tyler, I said I would make it worth your while if you came here this weekend, and I intend on doing just that. I would like you to start hauling bank forms for me on the West Coast. It's a hundred thousand-dollar a month account for you. I need a good trucking company I can count on to deliver these forms on time. Are you interested in something like that?"

"Thanks, Mr. Wentworth. Yes, I'd love to have the account."

"All right then, consider it done. I'll have an account executive meet with your people to work out all the details. It's a pleasure doing business with you. Enjoy yourself today." Martin stood up and offered his hand.

Cole shook Martin Wentworth's hand and walked back down the hall. He found Derek sipping a drink outside the library.

"Good news?" Derek asked Cole.

"We just got another big account."

Derek smiled at Cole and gave him a pat on the shoulder. "That's great."

Cole starred off and looked completely lost. "I'm not sure if it is or not."

Derek looked confused. "Why would you say that?"

"I'm quickly being pulled into the Wentworth's world. I'm not sure I can stop it now even if I wanted to."

11

THE GIRLS FINALLY pulled themselves away from the country music star and the four of them left for the barbecue. It was time to see what kind of party the Wentworth's could throw.

It was a warm and humid day, so they walked to the tents to escape the hot sun. Each tent held a different event inside. Wine tasting in one and Western art in another. Cole figured that six to seven hundred people had to be at the barbecue already.

Country music filled the air and some people danced.

The local Indians had six teepees' set up. They beat drums, sang chants, and performed tribal dances in elaborate costumes.

Several cowboys practiced in the arena for the rodeo.

After sampling a variety of foods and walking around a few hours, they sat down where the stage was set up. Cole knew Jan didn't want to miss a minute of Trevor Jackson's show.

A man in a Western cut suit adjusted the microphone before he spoke on stage. The sound carried through speakers placed around the whole ranch. "Folks, if I could have your attention for a few minutes, I'd like to introduce the gentleman responsible for all of this today. He is the founder and president of our great company."

Everyone there applauded and whistled. When the applause died down, he continued.

"And what's even more amazing, he finds a way to make this barbecue bigger every year. I give you the man who throws the best damn barbecue on the planet. Not to mention, he signs all of our paychecks. Ladies and gentleman, Mr. Martin Wentworth!"

Applause filled the arena as if he was everyone's hero. A lot of people stood up and whistled.

Martin shook the man's hand, stepped to the microphone, and waited for the applause to die down.

Cole could tell he loved every second of it.

Martin controlled the crowd. "Thank you all for coming today and I do make this barbecue a little bigger every year. But that's the way we do things in Texas."

The crowd cheered and whistled again.

"You know how you can tell if a Texan is happy? When his belly is full of Southern barbecue and he's got lots of stories to tell about it."

The crowd laughed and clapped some more.

Martin smiled and continued. "The people of Texas are very special to me. I love this great state with all my heart and soul. Texas is one of the most powerful states in the union. That's why when we elect a governor; we want him to be strong. We want him to speak our minds how ever bold we might think our ideas are. We demand to be heard and expect the people who represent us to carry our message the way that we would say it from our own lips. We want a strong man who's not afraid to stand up for Texans."

There was more applause and whistles from the crowd.

"Now I don't know about you, but not too many men I know fit that description. But there is one man here today that does. This man was born and raised in Texas. He knows our ways, our needs, and our goals. I believe he will give this state the recognition that we demand and deserve. When you find a man like that, you should thank the good Lord that he's on our side. Ladies and gentleman, I give you our governor of the great state of Texas, Governor Dexter Simms!"

The applause grew intense when the young governor walked out on stage and shook Martin's hand. He whispered a word of thanks to him and started his talk.

Katherine stood where Martin came off stage. "Well daddy, I see you managed to get your puppet boy in office. My, what a tragic loss it was for Texas when Governor Manning disappeared. I'll bet you're all broke up over that."

"That's none of your concern now is it, darlin'?"

"No I guess nothing you do is. I mean, you shut me out of everything else. Speaking of that, where's Marty today?"

"I was hoping you could tell me," Martin said, looking around.

"I don't have any idea. He's going to make a wonderful president for Texmar. He's so darn dependable."

"Give it a rest, sweetheart. I've heard this more times than I care to think about. However, I would like to see you Monday morning in my office to discuss a few things."

"You can count on me being there. I hope you can find Marty by then. After all, shouldn't the future president of

Texmar be here for such an important meeting?" Katherine walked away.

Just then, an arm came around her shoulder and Jake gave her a big kiss on the lips. "Hey, I wondered where you were."

"I was just talking to daddy."

"I hope you didn't make him mad. I need to talk business with him."

"Jake, my father and I tolerate each other. We never get along, so get used to it."

"I just don't think that's any way to act toward your father."

"Let me get something straight, sweetheart. My relationship with my father is not your concern, and if we're going to get along, you're going to have to stay out of it. Likewise, your business with my father is not my concern. Are we clear on that?"

"God, you're such a wild woman. I ought to make hot, steamy love to you right here on the ground." He smiled at her and she returned one. "Come on, let's go get something to eat."

Cole and Jan listened to Trevor Jackson when he saw Katherine and Jake walk by. She looked so incredible, but seeing her with Jake made him wish he could have met her before she became engaged.

The next morning it was almost sunrise. Cole was up at four thirty making coffee. He had to see one last sunrise before he went back to Southern California. He sipped his coffee and waited for the magic to dazzle him one more time.

He thought he was dreaming when he saw Katherine walking her horse towards the guesthouse. But when he heard her voice, he realized it wasn't a dream at all.

"Mornin'," she said, holding the reins of the dark brown horse.

Just her presence made him feel good. "This is becoming a habit with us."

She smiled at him. "Ain't it great?"

He looked in her beautiful blue eyes. "Yes it is. Come to invite me on another wild adventure?"

"I'm a little crazy sometimes but I'll probably out grow it one day."

"I hope not. I kind of like you the way you are."

"I didn't want you to leave without saying how much I enjoyed meeting you."

"For some reason, I don't feel like I want to say good bye to you."

"Then don't, Cole. I want you to come back."

"Is that an invitation?"

“You don’t need an invitation to come back here, cowboy.” She looked serious.

He got goose bumps from the look she gave him. “Thanks, Katherine. I’d love to come back to see you and this beautiful ranch again. I want to see that hotel of yours one day too.”

“Oh, you will. I give you my personal guarantee on it. It’ll be a long, hard road to get there, but isn’t that half the fun of it? Promise me you’ll come back, Cole.” Katherine took his hand, pulled him towards her, and kissed him on the lips. Without anything else said, she mounted her horse and rode away.

12

KATHERINE WOKE UP early Monday morning to another spectacular sunrise at the Southern Star Ranch. But it didn't seem as special as it did over the weekend. Without Cole there, she felt empty and lost. How could she have these kinds of feelings when Jake was going to marry her? She thought.

She walked to the kitchen and poured herself a cup of coffee.

Her mother came in dressed in her gardening clothes. Amanda Wentworth didn't let too many people see her like that. "Up a little early this morning aren't you, sweetheart?" She kissed her daughter on the cheek.

"I've got a lot on my mind, mama."

"Walk with me to the garden."

Amanda and Katherine walked out a side door of the house down a long, brick walkway to a large greenhouse.

Katherine opened the greenhouse door.

Amanda looked her daughter in the eye. "Honey, I know when something is troubling you so just tell me what it is."

Katherine drank a little of her coffee and thought about how much she should tell her mother. "You know I'm not going anywhere in Texmar and I'm not happy about that. I have a lot to offer the company, but daddy just ignores me most of the time."

"Did you ever think your father might be protecting you from something? I know he doesn't always operate the company according to the letter of the law." Amanda's Texas accent was more noticeable than Katherine's was.

"The real issue is he's grooming Marty to be president of Texmar. Even though Marty doesn't have what it takes to run the company?"

"So what are you going to do about it? I know you aren't the type to take this lying down."

"It hasn't been an easy decision but I've decided to leave Texmar and go off on my own."

"Are you sure that's what you want to do?"

"It's time to move on, mama. It's time for me to make my mark."

Amanda smiled at her daughter. "Well, I guess you have a little of your daddy in you. When we first met he was so ambitious and there was so much he wanted to accomplish. No one was going to stop him and the people who tried were amazed at how driven he was. It seemed to give him more strength when he had to overcome great obstacles. I guess you inherited that from him."

"Mama, but this is something I have to do."

"Dear, just tell your father your plans just like you told me. Even though he may not approve of the idea, deep down he'll understand. He'll understand you've got ambition and will fight for what you believe in no matter what. If it's something you have to do, then do it. Don't let life pass you by without fulfilling your dreams."

"I'm going to tell him today. I'm a little nervous about it."

"Are you sure that's all that's bothering you, honey?"

Katherine looked at her mother and wondered how much she knew about Cole. She gave her a big hug. "Well, that's all that I want to talk about right now." Katherine walked towards the door.

"Remember, be strong and stand up for yourself. Your father will use any weaknesses against you. He'll respect you more for being a fighter."

"Thanks, mama."

Katherine wiped a tear and kissed her as she left the greenhouse.

Martin opened his office door and gave his daughter a big hug. "Good morning, sweetheart. Like always, right on time."

Katherine was dressed in a dark blue business suit. Her long blond hair was neatly styled in a professional look. She put her briefcase down and sat in a large leather chair in front of Martin's desk. She was nervous but didn't let it show. Now, more than ever, she had to be strong. "I guess by now you know everything I'll be talking about today."

Martin looked surprised. "What makes you say that?"

Katherine smiled and shook her head. "Daddy, just how stupid do you think I am? Do you really think I don't know about your meetings with Austin?"

Martin smiled. "Wow! I've got to say I'm impressed."

"You have someone spy on your own family? You want Marty to be president of Texmar. Have you lost it?"

“I can’t help it if all of my business decisions aren’t popular with you. I know you think that you should be behind this desk. Maybe I’m not convinced of that.”

“Then let me prove it. Let me show you I can run Texmar.”

“Sweetheart, we’ve been over this many times before.”

Katherine stood up and walked to the window. “I know we have, and every time I get the same response. You see, daddy, you leave me no choice. You’ll never give me a chance to prove how good I am. And you know what, it’s your loss.” She felt a tear coming but held it back.

“I want you to be involved with the company, honey, but I don’t think you should run it. You can’t imagine what I have to do to keep this company profitable. It takes a lot out of you to stay on top. Now one day, when you give me that grandson I’ve always wanted, I’ll promise you he’ll be president. Mark my word on that.”

“So that’s it! This whole thing is about me being a woman? The whole thing is about your male ego?”

“Truthfully, darlin’ I don’t think a woman should hold the top position in this company. It’s not the image I want to project.”

“Let me tell you something. Just because my reproductive organs are on the inside instead of the outside doesn't mean I can't handle running Texmar! I thought you were smarter than that, daddy!"

"You're over reacting, sweetheart."

"So you would rather have Marty as president because he's a man. Is that right? I want to be clear on this because that is something I can't change." She looked him in the eye.

Martin looked away and then back at her. "I'm doing what I believe is right, and it's my decision to make Marty president. One day, he will grow up to be a fine business man. He's still young and has to get a few things out of his system."

"Daddy, I can't keep fighting a losing battle with you. I have too much ambition to be kept on a short leash. I'm of no use to you if you won't let me present my ideas. I can really help this company and I'm sorry you can't see that. So I'm through with all of it."

"Don't do anything crazy, sweetheart. You're upset and that's not the time to make a rational decision."

"You think I haven't thought this thing through? I've been fighting with you over this for twelve years. I wish I had known the way you felt about women a long time ago. I wouldn't have wasted so much time here. I'll type up a formal resignation as soon as I get back to my office."

"You're throwing away a good career."

"No, I blew a good career when I came to work for you. Do yourself a favor though. Stay out of my business affairs. If I hear about you threatening my business partners again, you'll be dealing with my thugs."

"What, you mean that little hotel project on the island?"

"I mean if I want Leo Mariano to be my partner, then that's my business. I don't want him being threatened by your goons."

"You think that hotel will ever make a nickel of profit?"

Katherine walked toward the door. "Like I said, stay away from my business."

"That's a big bite to take for your first deal. Tell you what I will do. I'll buy the island from you and you'll have start up money for something that will actually make money."

"Now why would you want to do that? You don't do anything unless it benefits you or the company. Not a chance."

"Then let me be your partner and we can finance the deal together," Martin said.

He was too anxious and Katherine saw him struggle for control. She didn't know why but she knew she had something he wanted. "You think after the way you treated me, I would even consider you as a partner. Besides, I plan on having a lot of women working for me and I don't think your ideas would fit in."

"I have ways of getting things moving quickly when it comes to licenses and permits."

"No! I want no part of you or Texmar in my business. I don't know why you're so interested in my island but I'm warning you right now to stay away from it." Katherine opened the door and was gone before Martin could say anything else.

He stood up from his desk, let out a big sigh and poured himself another cup of coffee.

Matt knocked on Martin's door and entered the office. "That looked like it went well."

"Better shut the door. We have to talk."

Before Matt shut the door, Marty pushed on it and entered the office.

"Well, look who we have here." Martin watched his son head for the bar.

"I know. Give me the speech. I'm expecting it."

"I hope she was worth it, son. You amaze me sometimes but we'll deal with that later. Right now we have to figure out how to stop your sister from building that hotel on the island. Both of you realize we can't allow that to happen. So let's put our heads together and figure out how we can stop her."

To everyone's surprise, the next thing out of Marty's mouth actually made sense. "Well, I would take something from her and use it as a bargaining chip."

Martin grinned and looked pleased. "You might just have something there, son. I knew your Wentworth blood would kick in one day."

"What about Jake? She would be pretty upset if he disappeared for awhile," Matt said, from the other side of the office.

Martin looked out the window. "No, I like him and Katherine doesn't get that attached to her men. I know that sounds crazy but it's true."

Marty spoke up again, "Hey, what about her friend, Wendy?"

Martin again looked surprised that his son actually had another good idea. "You're on a roll today, Marty. That's what we'll do. She loves her like a sister. Matt set it up with Austin today. Get the girl and we'll hold her until Katherine comes around to our way of thinking."

"Kinda' risky don't you think, Martin? I mean, what do we do with the girl if Katherine does come around?" Matt said, concerned.

"She won't even know we're involved. We can kidnap her one-day and invite her to dinner the next. That's the beauty of it." Martin walked over to Marty. "Welcome to the big leagues, son. I knew you had it in you. Then we all agree that we bargain with the girl. Matt, be sure Austin only uses people that are unfamiliar to her and our name is never used. She wears a hood the entire time. Otherwise if she knows we are involved she dies."

13

COLE ARRIVED AT Tyler Transport at seven a.m. on Monday, prepared for a busy day. When he reached the office, Alicia handed him a stack of mail. He called Agent Walker and set up a meeting so they wouldn't have to discuss anything on the phone. Next, he called Derek into the office. Eventually, he had to let him know what was going on.

Derek came in and talked about the trip to Houston. They talked for a few minutes before Cole decided to spill the beans. He felt like he owed it to Derek.

"Derek, there was something discussed in Martin Wentworth's office that I think you should know about."

Derek swallowed hard and looked at Cole like he knew what he was going to tell him. "Tell me it's good news."

"He wants to buy Tyler Transport."

Derek was silent for a minute and looked at Cole with a blank stare. "So what did you tell him?"

"He made me an offer and I told him I would think about it. But if the offer becomes more realistic, I might consider it. I want you to know what's going on. We've been through thick and thin together, and I'm not about to keep you in the dark on anything. This doesn't leave the office though. You're the only person who knows about it."

"Sure, but why are you even considering this? We came through some rough times, but now business is great. Why sell it now? I don't understand."

"I'm not sure I do either. I've got to do some serious thinking about this."

Derek stood up and made his way to the door. "Let me know what you decide."

"Hey, don't be mad about this. I don't plan on parting ways with you. No matter what I might do, I want you on my team. Okay?"

Derek nodded his head and left with a disappointing look.

Cole poured himself a cup of coffee and told Alicia to send in Garret Lane and Kyle Chambers. Each of them joined Cole for coffee and another meeting was under way.

"Kyle, what did you think about the Southern Star Ranch?," Cole sipped his hot coffee.

"It has got to be one of the finest pieces of property I've ever seen."

"Maybe I should have gone too," Garrett said, looking over Kyle's notes.

"So, did you find out anything interesting while you were there?" Cole took another drink of his coffee.

"Yes I did. Martin always has his scrambler on while he is in his office and his office at home. That's the little black box like this one." Kyle pointed to the small box on Cole's desk.

"It makes it impossible to listen in with bugs or long range microphones, right?" Cole looked at the box.

"Correct. Martin is careful what he says and where he says it so no one can find out what he's up to. However, when he's outside, he is the most vulnerable. That's when I picked up on some interesting conversation. He wants to buy your company right?"

"Yes he does."

"He talked to his brother, Matthew about going to eighty five million if he had to. He said if you refused at that amount, he would take control of your accounts and force you into the sale."

"So this guy gets what he wants no matter what?"

"I won't lie to you about Martin Wentworth. He'll roll over anyone who gets in his way. He's got the money and knows all of the right people to make things happen. He keeps a lot of shady characters on his payroll. People fear him because of his power."

Cole looked at his watch. "Anything else?"

"That's all I have for now."

"Great job, Kyle. Keep a close watch on Mr. Wentworth and let me know what else you turn up."

Cole shook hands with both of them before they left.

Alicia buzzed his phone and told him it was time to meet with Agent Walker. He felt like he needed the drive.

The ride on the sixty freeway took twenty minutes and the surface streets to the hotel took about the same amount of time.

He valet parked his Mercedes SL and walked to the coffee shop. He didn't spot the FBI Agent, so he waited at a table where he could see him walk in. He ordered a soft drink from the waitress and told her he was expecting someone.

When the waitress came back with his drink, she smiled at him and hurried off to her next table.

A man he didn't recognize stopped at his table and Cole's blood ran cold for a moment.

"Mr. Tyler, my name is Justin Wentworth."

The young man was six feet tall, on the slender side, and had a slight southern accent. He was casually dressed and well groomed. He sat down without taking his eyes off of Cole.

Cole didn't want him to see he was shocked by his presence so he did his best to act calm. "I'm meeting someone in a few minutes but you have my attention for now. What can I do for you, Justin?"

"Agent Walker will be a little late. He had electrical problems with his car." He seemed sure of himself.

Cole wondered where he got his information. "You seem to know a lot about my situation, Justin, but I know nothing about you."

"I'll give you the short version because I don't have much time. I'm Martin Wentworth's oldest son. I grew up at the Southern Star Ranch. My father groomed me all my life to run Texmar, but I didn't want any part of it. I tried to convince him I didn't want the job, but he wouldn't listen. My father and I butted heads over the issue for years. Finally I got fed up and one day I just left and never went back. His greed and obsession for power was something I couldn't stomach. I decided living my life like that wasn't worth living at all.

"I dated a gal that worked with computers and found them fascinating. I spent a few years writing and designing programs. I found that I had a knack for it. The little black box that Kyle brings with him every time he comes to see you. The same one my father uses so no one can eavesdrop on him. I invented it."

"How is it that you know so much about what I'm doing?" Cole was intrigued.

"Mr. Tyler, you have no idea what can be done with electronic knowledge. I invented the little black box so people could talk about business without the fear of someone listening in on them or steal their trade secrets." Justin never looked away from Cole.

"I'm still in the dark about how you know so much about what I'm doing. I used your black box at every meeting, even at my house."

"Remember, I invented it. That means I can also decode it and I'm the only one who can. In the wrong hands that could be dangerous."

"Okay, I'll buy that, but why are you telling me this?"

"I want to help my sister, Katherine. She's going to need all the help she can get when she takes on my father."

Now he had Cole's full attention. "Katherine's a pretty tough woman when it comes to business from what I've heard. What makes you think she needs any help?"

"She'll need it. My father won't allow her to build the hotel on her island."

"Okay, how do I fit into all of this?"

"I want to give you information on my father's plans before it happens."

Cole studied the young man for a moment. The whole thing seemed a little weird. "Why me, Justin?"

"Whether you know it or not, Katherine trusts you. There's one catch to all of this. I don't want her to know that I'm helping her. She likes to do things on her own. Katherine can be very stubborn sometimes."

Cole looked at his face and found no expression. He couldn't read this guy. "What makes you think your father will keep her from building her hotel?"

"It's not the hotel that he cares about. It's the island, Mr. Tyler."

Justin stood up and reached for his sunglasses.

Cole had a hundred more questions for him. "Where are you going, Justin?"

"Think about what I said. I'll talk to you again soon. Tell no one what was said here today." He walked away and was gone as quick as he came.

Cole was left at the table speechless and couldn't believe what had just taken place. He saw Agent Walker coming toward him. Justin had timed his exit perfectly.

Agent Walker saw Cole looking off into space. He looked around the room looking for anything unusual. "Sorry I'm late I had car problems. Mr. Tyler, are you all right? You look like you've seen a ghost."

Cole watched Justin walk out of the hotel. "Maybe I just did."

14

AT SIX-THIRTY p.m., Katherine arrived at the Phoenix Marriot hotel and walked quickly to Tony Delisle's seminar. She saw the sign in front of the open door that advertised Tony's seminar. When she entered, she sat behind a hundred people seated in the large meeting room. She listened to him talk to the crowd. He reminded Katherine of a minister speaking to his congregation.

"When you came here tonight, you were looking for a change in your life. You have heard from countless people who have benefited from this valuable information. You learned from our short time together that life is all about making the right decisions. Now, you have to make a decision. Is it going to be to walk out that door tonight and live your life like you always have? You came here because you were ready for a change. So, it seems to me, that is not the right choice to make.

"Or, are you going to make the right decision and take control of your life? Let me show you how to be happy. Let me show you how to be successful. If you follow the information on these DVDs, I guarantee you will live a much more rewarding life. Don't cheat yourself out of a life you could have had.

"I've got ten million people who agree with me. These people were just like you. The only difference is they have applied this information to their lives. The information on these disks are the blueprints you need to live that life. You can be happy, you can be healthy, and you can be successful. Let me show you how.

"Some of you are already getting up to purchase this information in the back of this room. Every remaining day of your life will be better for it.

"I want to thank you for your time, and I want to give you all something for coming tonight. If you decided not to purchase now, I want to give you our eight hundred number. My staff will help you with any problem you might have in your life. It's my way of giving something back to so many people who have given me so much. I wish you all a happy, healthy, and prosperous life."

Everyone applauded when Tony came off the small stage. Several people lined up to purchase his products.

After a few minutes, he saw Katherine sitting in the back row of the room. He walked in her direction and spread his arms out to her. "How long has it been Texas Lady?" Tony gave her a big hug and a kiss on the lips.

He was dressed in an expensive suit and was as good looking as she remembered. "Too long. I see you haven't lost your touch convincing people to part with their money."

He smiled. "Hey, let's find a place to talk."

Tony led her to an office in the hotel not far from where the meeting room was. He pulled out a chair for her and offered her a drink.

"Sure, I'll have a tequila. Tony, I came here on business."

"Damn, I thought you might want to jump my bones or something."

"Well, my fiancée might not approve of that."

"Never stopped you before. Besides, I won't tell him." He handed her the drink and showed his beautiful white teeth. "Can't blame a guy for trying can you?"

She smiled at him and took the drink.

He sat next to her. “So, what kind of business?”

“I’m going to build a hotel on my island and I thought you might want a piece of it. It’s a killer deal, Tony, with lots of profit for a few to share.”

“How many millions do I have to part with?”

“Total cost is 500 hundred million, and I’m putting up half. The rest is open.” Katherine sipped her drink without looking at him.

“Ordinarily, I pay high priced experts who make these decisions for me. But sometimes you have to go with your gut feeling. How much for me to buy in?”

“I want as few partners as possible. I’m only looking to make a few people filthy rich.” Katherine held her breath. It sounded like Tony was interested.

“Okay, put me down for 20.”

Katherine was pleased, but knew she could get more, now that he agreed to get in on the deal. She decided to push knowing it was a gutsy move. “Tony, I need major players on this one. I only want two partners at the most.”

Tony poured them another drink. Almost thirty seconds went by before he broke the silence. “You’re asking me to spend millions on a project that I know anything about?”

“You have to trust me on this one.”

He studied her with his deep brown eyes. "If you have dinner with me tonight, I might be in a more generous mood."

Katherine bent over the table, and gave him a big kiss on the lips. She looked deep in his eyes. "I promise you we'll both make a lot of money."

"Okay I'm in for 50?"

"How about 100 and we'll have desert in your room after dinner?"

"You're a tough broad when it comes to business."

"I'm trying to make you richer."

"What about your fiancée?"

"You said you wouldn't tell."

"Okay, lady, a hundred million dollars, and you have a partner. Now let's go up to my suite. I just spent a fortune and that always makes me horny."

"As soon as I have your check, I'll take care of that."

15

KATHERINE PARKED HER Mercedes SL 550, in the circle drive at the ranch, and her mother hurried out to meet her. "I'm so glad to see you, honey." Amanda hugged her daughter when she got out of the car.

"You know me, mom. I can't stay away very long."

"I know you must be feeling terrible about everything. Why don't you come in and we'll talk about it."

"Mom, I don't feel bad at all. In fact, I feel relieved I left Texmar. Now I can do what ever I want. Let's go inside and I'll tell you all about my new hotel."

"Honey, you don't know what's happened do you?"

Katherine looked at her mother and braced for bad news. "What happened, mama?"

"Wendy has disappeared. No one has heard anything from her for two days."

Katherine gasped for breath. "No! What happened?"

The next hour, Amanda filled her daughter in on the details of how Wendy disappeared without a trace.

Just then her father came through the front door and glared at her. "Real shame about your friend, sweetheart. I hope she's all right." He walked into the kitchen, opened the refrigerator door, and hid his face.

Katherine quickly walked into the kitchen. "Daddy, would you care to see me in your office for a minute? I want to discuss something with you."

Martin looked up from the refrigerator, shut the door, and smiled at her. "Why sure, darlin'. I always have time for my little girl."

She followed him to the office and realized she had to get control of her emotions. The door shut and she starred him down like a lion about to pounce upon its prey. "You don't fool me, daddy. I know you're a better actor than that. What did you do with Wendy?"

"It's pretty simple, darlin'. Sell me the island and your little friend goes untouched. But if you continue to build the hotel, we start mailing her to her husband a piece at a time." He didn't even flinch when he said it.

"What is it about that damn island?"

"You can build ten hotels somewhere else, but I don't want one on that island."

"What makes you think I would sell you my island after doing something like this?"

"Honey, I don't give a hoot in hell what you think. I won't allow you to put that hotel up. I'll use all my power to stop you." He looked at his daughter with cold, dead serious eyes.

"I'm out of Texmar now. So why are you doing this?"

"You have my terms; you don't need to know any more."

Katherine took a deep breath and thought for a moment. "No deal. If I have to sacrifice Wendy for my hotel, then that's the way it has to be. She's an acceptable casualty." She walked to the door and her father barely caught her before she made one of her fast exits.

Martin raised his voice. "I won't let you build that damn hotel!"

Katherine responded before she left the office. “I told you not to mess with me and my hotel. Now, you have to deal with the consequences.”

“You have no idea what I could do to you, do you?. But you’re about to find out. Consider your friend dead.”

16

MARTIN HAD HIS feet up drinking a whiskey in his office after a long day. When his private line rang, he thought it might be one of his lady friends. But he knew it was trouble when Antonio Viatsi came on the line.

"Wentworth, we gotta' talk. I need to explain a few things to you." Viatsi spoke with a heavy Italian accent.

"Well, hello to you too, Antonio. How did you get this number?"

"It doesn't matter. I wanna' talk."

"Must be serious. You usually try your best to avoid me," Martin said.

"Meet me at my place tomorrow and we'll get a few things straight."

"I'd have to be pretty stupid to do that, don't you think? How about I land my helicopter in front of your place about noon? You bring one bodyguard and I'll have one on board. We'll do our talking away from the arsenal you keep at your house. I don't like surprises and neither do you."

"Okay, but I only want to see one man and the pilot in that chopper or I don't get in."

"My helicopter only holds four people with a pilot and co-pilot. Just be ready tomorrow at noon, and we'll have your chat. You have yourself a nice day now." Martin hung up the phone. He knew Austin would know what to do.

At eleven thirty the next day, the helicopter took off from the top of the Wentworth building with the pilot, Martin, and Austin.

When the helicopter came down on the Viatsi estate lawn, Martin saw ten men with automatic rifles guarding the perimeter.

One of them opened the side door and looked around the cabin. The wind from the helicopter blades blew in with extreme force. He motioned the okay, and Antonio emerged from his home with one bodyguard as agreed.

Both men got inside, and the helicopter rose back in the air. Antonio and his bodyguard both looked at Martin with looks that could kill.

Martin broke the silence. "Well, what the hell is so important that you drag me out here in the middle of nowhere. I'm a busy man."

Viatsi stared at him with hatred. "You killed my nephew, Michael. Why?"

Martin acted calm and in control. "Who said I killed him?"

"Don't insult me, Wentworth. I asked why?"

"Okay, he was selling drugs to my son. I warned him more than once but he wouldn't listen."

"You should have come to me and I would have taken care of it."

"Wrong answer, Antonio. It was my business and you had nothing to do with it."

"This was my brother's boy. You killed him like an animal. They picked up his body parts and put them in a bag!" Antonio's voice got louder. "I had to tell my brother there was nothing left of his boy. His mother wept for weeks and I couldn't say anything to comfort her. You mutilated him and you hurt my family, and you will pay the price."

Viatsi's bodyguard sized Austin up.

Martin pointed his finger at Antonio. "Now you listen, I take care of business swiftly and if someone gets in my way, I get rid of them. I'm not in the habit of asking your permission to eliminate a problem. Your nephew was a dope pusher. It's not a very safe profession."

"You think nothing will come of this? You think you can live your life like this never happened? You are wrong! Michael was Sicilian and his death will be avenged! It is a matter of honor, no matter how long it takes."

"Well, I'm sorry to hear you say that. See I can't have people threatening me like that, Antonio. It isn't good for my image. I suppose you would like your bodyguard to shoot me now. Is that the plan?"

Antonio's bodyguard reached inside his coat, but before he could produce a weapon, a pop came from behind his seat. He yelled out in pain, slumped over, and leaned against the window.

Austin held a pistol to Viatsi's head before he could grasp what was happening. He reached inside of Antonio's coat and pulled a pistol from it.

Martin looked at the dead body then at Antonio. "I guess you have to watch who you threaten now days, don't you? Did you really think I was going to let you leave after that speech you just gave me? I figure it's you or me, Antonio, and I'm not done living yet. So, I guess that leaves just you.

"If you kill me, this will not be over. Where I come from, we live by honor and tradition. You will pay if I die or not."

"Well, you got me shaking in my boots. You're nothing but trash to me now. Throw out the trash, Austin."

Austin opened up the side door of the helicopter and the air rushed in. He threw out the bodyguard first, and then grabbed Antonio.

"You will be killed for this Wentworth! Not even you can escape our ways of justice!"

Martin motioned to Austin and he pushed Antonio out the door.

17

THE HELICOPTER LANDED on the heliport on the Texmar building and Martin and Austin entered the building through a private entrance.

Once they reach Martin's office, they saw a large bag hanging from the ceiling by a chain.

Austin immediately drew his gun and looked the office over. The bag looked like a black body bag from the morgue.

"Let's have a look, Austin." Martin said, not knowing what might await them.

Austin checked for booby traps, untied the top of the bag, and looked inside. "Oh my God! Its Marty!"

"What? Marty's in there? Is he alive?" Martin walked closer.

"Mr. Wentworth, can you help me lift the bag off of the hook? Then we can lay him on the floor."

Martin helped lift the bottom of the bag so the weight was off of the hook.

Austin unhooked the bag, and the two of them laid it on the floor. Austin unzipped the bag and found Marty unconscious. He put his hand on Marty's neck. "He's got a pulse."

"Thank God! I'll call for an ambulance. Better yet, let's put him in the helicopter and fly him to the trauma center."

"Good idea. I'll call the pilot back." Austin dialed the phone.

They both carried Marty's limp body to the helicopter.

It landed six minutes later at a hospital where Martin had donated enough millions to have a wing named after him.

After they got him to emergency Martin paced in a private waiting room with Austin. "You know what I can't quite figure out, Austin. How did someone get through all of the security and into my office in broad daylight? Something doesn't add up here."

"Those are rolling codes. They change every thirty seconds. It's virtually impossible."

Martin starred out the window. "Yet someone did it. I've always considered my office a fortress. I can't have this happening especially now. Let's get a more sophisticated system and let's do it now."

"I'll get right on it. In the meantime, any idea who might do something like this?"

"The Viatsi Family would be my first guess. After him, take your pick."

"Any one besides Viatsi give you a problem lately?"

"Well, Katherine quit the company you know. She didn't take the kidnapping very well either. She swore revenge on me unless I released her friend. But I don't think she has the resources to pull something off like this."

"Don't be so sure. Your daughter is a very smart woman and she is capable of more than you think. I wouldn't underestimate her."

"You give her too much credit, Austin."

At that moment, a nurse came in and Martin and Austin both rose to their feet.

"Gentlemen, if you will follow me this way."

The nurse led them down the hall to the chapel.

Martin lashed out at the nurse. "What's going on with my boy? I want some answers!"

"I'm sorry, sir, I was only instructed to bring you here. I don't know anything about your son."

"Well, you get someone here who does!"

"Someone is coming right in to brief you, sir. Please wait in here."

Martin and Austin entered the chapel and sat down.

"I don't know what to say, Mr. Wentworth."

"I want someone to tell me what the hell is going on with Marty."

Then, the chapel doors open, and a young orderly appeared. He looked frightened at Austin's sudden move to keep him away from Martin.

"What do you want, kid?" Austin grabbed him and backed him up against the wall.

The young orderly was shaking. He was struggling to get the words out of his mouth. "Some woman gave me twenty bucks to bring this up here."

Austin took the piece of paper the boy was holding and read it to Martin. "Listen to this. This is only a warning. An enemy could easily have killed Marty. He was drugged and will sleep it off. Release Wendy now. Your warnings are all used up." Austin handed the note to Martin.

They left the chapel, walked down the hall, and found the doctor.

Martin spoke before the doctor said anything. "He was drugged, wasn't he?"

The doctor looked surprised. "He'll be fine by tomorrow. How did you know that?"

Martin shook his head in disbelief and walked away. "Austin, keep an eye on my daughter. She's going to be trouble."

"If she broke the security codes, she's going to be more than trouble. What about her friend?"

"No one bullies me, especially my own daughter. I don't know how she pulled off this little plan of hers, but she's proving to be a better advisory than I thought. But let's see what she's really made of. Take her friend's left ring finger; cut it off with her wedding ring still on. Box it up and send it to her husband."

Martin boarded the helicopter with Austin and they left the hospital. As the helicopter rose into the air, Martin whispered, "The ball is back in your court, sweetheart."

18

AT SIX THIRTY p.m., the limousine pulled up in front of Cole Tyler's house. He and his attorney had been going over a stack of paperwork for the sale of Tyler Transport. They had been working for days, trying to get everything in order. Now it was time to leave for Houston, and any last minute papers would have to be faxed.

Cole grabbed his briefcase and loosened his tie before instructing the chauffeur to load the three black bags by the door. He shook his attorney's hand and hurried to the limo.

Cole decided to fix a scotch on the rocks from the small bar. Twenty-five minutes later, he was at the private hanger at Ontario airport. Within minutes, they were in the air flying towards Houston, Texas. The pilot told him it was two hours flying time and there was a call for him. Cole picked up the phone and heard a voice he had heard only once before.

"Mr. Tyler?"

"Yes," Cole answered.

"I spoke with you not long ago at a hotel. It was in the coffee shop where you met Agent Walker."

"I remember you."

"I would appreciate it if we could stay anonymous for our short conversation."

"How did you know...? Never mind. What can I do for you?"

"I want you to help my sister with a problem. Can I count on you to give her some information? It's important."

"Yes, whatever it is, I will help her."

"You'll find the information in your briefcase. Thanks, Cole, I knew I could count on you. We'll talk again soon."

The phone went dead.

Cole opened his briefcase and found the information. The message read: Cole, give Katherine this address. Be careful.

The address followed the message, but nothing else was on the paper.

The jet landed in Houston and another limo was waiting to take him to the Southern Star Ranch. The closer he got, the more excited he became.

The car pulled up to the guesthouse and Cole immediately recognized it. As soon as he opened the door, the phone rang.

"Mr. Tyler, how was your flight?"

"Very nice, Mr. Wentworth."

"Good, how bout' you and me taking a horseback ride tomorrow morning right after breakfast. Are you up for that?"

"Yes, I would love to take a ride."

"Okay then, I'll send Dean to pick you up at seven sharp."

"Sounds good. I'll be looking forward to it."

The next day the sun came up over the East Mountain, and Cole was ready for it. With coffee cup in hand and a nice warm jacket, he watched the spectacular event. It was just like he remembered and, as always, it was special for him. He halfway expected Katherine to come riding up, but today it didn't happen.

Dean arrived at six fifty five and drove Cole to the main barn of the ranch.

Cole and Martin got on two saddled horses and rode away. Within a few minutes, they trotted to a pasture on the West Side of the ranch.

They stopped the horses, and took in the breathtaking view before Martin spoke. "I come here sometimes to escape from the world. I know, hard to believe I'm human isn't it?" Martin patted the neck of his horse. "This ranch is the only thing I'm really proud of." Cole looked his way. "What about the empire you created? Surely, that was no small undertaking. You must be proud of all that you have accomplished."

"Not really. It's just a business and anyone can succeed in business. If you want to know the truth I envy you."

"Why would you envy me?"

"Well, once I pay you all that money for your company I only get bigger. But you get to start over again. For me Cole, it's the thrill of getting there. What I wouldn't give to wipe the slate clean again and start over from scratch. What an adventure, never knowing what will happen next."

Cole couldn't believe what he was hearing.

"What will you do with yourself once you sell the business, Cole?"

"I haven't had a lot of time to think about that. I've been busy lately."

"Then why don't you tell me how much your place is going to cost me."

"Now? Out here?"

"I can't think of a better place to make a deal. Hell I'm more generous when I'm out here anyway. A big fancy office is stuffy. Besides, it doesn't have near the view that we have here. Now how much do you want plain and simple?"

This was not the way that Cole had pictured this deal going down. "I spent twenty years of my life building that place. I sweated out the tough times, and in the beginning, I sacrificed my own salary so I would have enough money to make my payroll. It was rough for many years when I started out, but somehow I managed to make it through. The true market value, with all of the accounts, I figure is eighty three million. I want another two million to pay every employee I have a severance package. They stuck with me through thick and thin and I won't turn my back on them."

"Well, after that speech what am I supposed to say? You really do want me to pay through the nose for your company don't you?"

"It's worth every penny."

"I don't doubt that. I suppose I could give you a few good reasons to get you down five million or so. But I don't feel like arguing about it, so I'll give you your price. Consider it a deal." Martin smiled and shook his hand.

19

COLE AND MARTIN walked out of Martin's home office into the family room and saw Amanda Wentworth talking to two men.

"What's going on?" Martin surprised them with his harsh tone.

The men identified themselves as detectives. "Mr. Wentworth, we're sorry to disturb you but we want to ask you and your wife about a missing person."

Martin frowned. "Okay, ask away."

"We're investigating the disappearance of Wendy Taggert. She vanished a few days ago, and until today, we didn't have any leads."

"And what did you discover today?" Martin looked unhappy with the news.

"Well, sir, her husband received her severed finger in the mail today. He identified her wedding ring on the finger. The odd part about it is, no ransom was requested. Frankly, we're stumped right now."

"I wish I could help you, detective, but we barely know the Taggert's," Martin said.

"If you can think of anything that might help us we would appreciate a call." He handed Martin his card.

"Absolutely. We'll give you a call if we hear anything at all."

The detectives left and Martin excused himself and left the room.

Cole asked Mrs. Wentworth about the disappearance of Wendy and she filled him in on what was going on. They talked for ten minutes before he decided to ask about Katherine.

"Mrs. Wentworth, do you know where I might find Katherine?"

"She said she was going to see Wendy's husband and children. She grew up with her you know. She feels so bad about what happened to her. They're more like sisters than friends. The Taggert's own the ranch next door."

"Mrs. Wentworth, I need to talk to Katherine and it's important that I get to her as soon as possible."

"Of course. I'll have a car brought around for you." She picked up the phone and dialed some numbers. "A car will be in the driveway waiting for you in a couple of minutes."

"Thanks, Mrs. Wentworth." Cole felt the piece of paper in his pocket. He remembered Justin saying it was important, but now he knew how important it might be.

Within minutes, the car was brought up and a ranch hand gave him directions to the Taggert ranch.

Cole sped off and was in the Taggert's ranch driveway in ten minutes. He rushed to the Taggert's door and rang the bell. When the door opened, he found himself face to face with Katherine. He got goose bumps when he saw her.

"My God, Cole, what on Earth are you doing here?" She hugged him.

"I have something I think is important."

"Come in and let's talk."

"I would love to any other time, but I need you to come with me now." He closed the door and gave her the piece of paper.

She looked puzzled. "It's an address. I don't get it."

"I don't either, but I think it's important that we check that address out."

Without hesitation, the two of them got in the car and sped away. The address belonged to a dark and vacant warehouse.

Katherine made a phone call to the detective working the case.

The police showed up a few minutes later and stayed away far enough so they still had the element of surprise. They told Cole and Katherine to stay back in case they had to fire shots.

After the police surrounded the building, it was time to make their move.

Katherine hung on tight to Cole.

The lock on the door was snapped and the police rushed in. Several gunshots rang out, and Cole and Katherine held each other a little tighter. They could see shadows of people running and heard a lot of yelling until the shots finally stopped.

Cole peeked his head up so he could see.

Katherine looked at Cole with hope in her eyes.

Then, a detective brought out a man in handcuffs. Then, two more men followed, in handcuffs.

An ambulance pulled up to the door and the two attendants rolled a gurney inside.

Katherine let go of Cole's hand and quickly ran for the warehouse.

Cole followed her still shaken from what had just happened. He saw the ambulance attendants wheeling the gurney with a woman covered up to her neck with a blanket.

Katherine held Wendy's hand and talked with her as they put her in the ambulance.

Wendy spoke to Katherine, obviously shaken by the ordeal. "They.... They.... They cut my finger off. Why would they do that to me? Why would they...." Her face was filled with tears as they put her in the ambulance.

Katherine came over to Cole and hugged him. "I don't know how you got that information, but thanks for saving her. Please don't leave town before I get a chance to talk with you." She got into the ambulance and it drove away.

20

AT A LITTLE after ten a.m., Martin, Matt, Marty, and Austin gathered in Martin's office.

Martin was beaming like a young kid who had just got laid for the first time. "Okay, gentleman. Today we're going to the island to undo anything Katherine has started. We'll have a little fun with her but nothing serious."

Matt had a steaming cup of coffee in his hand. "What's the story with Katherine, now that her friend has been released? Is she going to be trouble for us?"

"I can deal with her. Don't let her ruin our plans." Martin was confident about it.

"Yah, she's just playing the part of a real tough woman. She's no match for us," Marty said.

"She's a real threat and you had all better wake up to it," Austin said. "Don't take her lightly, Mr. Wentworth. She found out where the Taggert girl was in just a few days. She drugged Marty, stuffed him in a bag, hung him up in your office, and got around your high tech security. I'd say she is being polite to you. She could have done a lot more."

"What about that, Martin. That's kind of amazing isn't it?" Matt asked.

Martin shook his head. "Listen to yourselves. Are you going to let her take control? She's not even in the same league as us. She's gotten lucky a couple of times and you're ready to throw in the towel. What do you think about it, Marty?"

"You guys are talking like losers. Never let a woman be in charge. Right, pop?" Marty was drinking bourbon.

Austin and Matt rolled their eyes.

"Look guys, I said I would handle it. Now we've got business to take care of and I won't allow anything to disrupt it. My daughter will back off with the right amount of pressure. I've got it all under control. Let's get to the helicopter and get over there," Martin said, leading the way to the heliport.

The helicopter took off a few minutes later with all four men inside.

The helicopter flew over the Gulf of Mexico, and fifteen minutes later, the island was in sight. The helicopter made a right turn toward the landing zone but held up when Katherine's voice filled the cabin.

"Good morning, gentlemen. I trust you all had a good flight over."

Martin turned pale and looked at the other three men.

Matt started to perspire through his expensive suit.

Marty said his usual "Oh shit."

Austin prepared for the worst but listened carefully.

Katherine continued. "I thought I warned you about messing with me and my island, daddy. Why don't you listen to my warnings? Either you think I'm stupid or you think I'm bluffing."

Martin responded. "Darlin', we don't give a goat's butt what you think. We'll do anything we like with you or your little island."

Ten seconds of silence passed and everyone looked tense.

Katherine spoke with confidence. "I'll give you one chance to leave before I teach you a lesson."

Martin decided to call her bluff. "What are you going to do, blow us out of the sky? I don't think you've got the guts."

The helicopter continued to hover off the coast of the island.

"Take my advice, gentlemen, this island is off limits to you. I'm warning you for the last time. Turn around and leave or face the consequences." She waited for a response.

"Pilot, land this helicopter now!" Martin ordered.

The pilot made a move to land but the controls didn't respond. The helicopter flew to open water a half-mile from the island and hovered a hundred feet above the water.

"Sir, I have no control over this helicopter!" The pilot yelled. "The controls are frozen. Somehow, she is controlling it!"

"Dammit, you better get control or you'll never fly again!" Martin raised his voice.

Katherine's voice came back into the speakers. "You have been repeatedly warned, so you leave me no choice. Remember, I could have done this at a thousand feet instead of a hundred feet."

The four men looked at each other. But when the engine shut down, they all knew what was next.

The helicopter fell from the sky and hit the water with a powerful impact. It filled with water quickly but they all had time to get out of their seat belts before it sank.

They all treaded water and debris from the helicopter floated to the surface.

Martin spit out water from his mouth. "Damn her! One helicopter gone!"

Matt looked disgusted. "That's all you've got to say is the damn helicopter is gone?"

"What a bitch! My sister's a bitch! I hope you can hear me!" Marty yelled.

"We're going to have to take her a little more seriously." Austin said.

Marty turned to his father. "I thought you said you had it under control, Pop?"

"God, please tell me I didn't hear that. You don't get it do you, moron? She caught us with our pants down. She out-smarted us and I give her a lot of credit for that. I wish you had half the brains that she has."

Then, they heard a boat coming towards them from a distance. When it got close the man cut the motor and drifted toward them.

"Some nice lady paid me to pick you boys up and take you back to the mainland."

21

WHEN AMANDA WENTWORTH gave a dinner party, it was serious business. She considered herself the greatest host in Houston. Many prominent people desired a seat at one of her dinner parties.

She had a new evening gown designed for her from a prominent designer in Texas. She slipped into her new gown carefully with help from the designer's assistant.

Martin slammed the front door and came up the stairs soaking wet. He gave her a nasty look. "Don't ask. I'll shower and change as fast I can."

Thirty minutes later, Martin came downstairs to see that Trevor Jackson and his date had arrived. The doorbell rang again and Matt and his wife came in. In a matter of twenty minutes, everyone was having drinks in the library.

Martin glared at Katherine a few times but hadn't spoken to her yet.

Jake started a conversation with Matt and Martin so Katherine made her way over to Cole.

As she walked toward him, dressed in a black gown, she put on her best smile. He was a good-looking man and Katherine found him hard to resist.

Cole excused himself from the magazine editor he was talking with and walked to one side of the room with Katherine.

She felt good next to him. "I'm still a little shaken up after finding Wendy yesterday."

Cole held a drink. "How is she doing anyway?"

"She'll recover eventually. Her emotional well being will take some time."

"I'm glad we found her before they did anything else. Why did they take her anyway?"

"It's complicated, Cole. There's a lot going on here that's hard to believe."

"Anything I might be able to help you with?"

She looked deep in his dark brown eyes and could tell that he was sincere. "Why do I feel this great chemistry between us?"

"You know what they say, don't mess with Mother Nature."

"Doing anything tomorrow morning?"

"That's a loaded question coming from you. What did you have in mind?"

"I want your opinion about something on the island. Will you come over with me tomorrow morning?"

"I can't think of anything else I'd rather do. Well, almost anything." He smiled at her.

"Okay then, I'll pick you up about eight tomorrow morning at your guesthouse. I better get back to Jake before he thinks we have something going." She winked at him.

When she was about half way across the room, Martin pulled her off to one side. "What the hell kind of stunt was that today?"

She shook free of his hold on her arm. "What's the matter, daddy, you can dish it out but you can't take it?"

"You are way out of line little girl. I could crush you any time I see fit."

"Didn't I warn you about messing with me? I'm only acting in defense. But if you want more then keep coming at me. I'm building that hotel on my island and nothing, including you, will stop me."

Martin drank from his glass. "You're in for more trouble than you can handle."

"Well then, you better hire more goons because I haven't even gotten mad yet. I would prefer to work with you instead of against you."

"Fine, then don't build that hotel."

"Give me one good reason why?"

He pointed his finger at her and started to walk away. "You have been warned." He turned his back.

"So have you!" She raised her voice.

Jake walked over and frowned at her. "I heard you trashed his helicopter today."

"Keep out of this, Jake."

"Hey, this is my business too, you know."

"How is it your business?"

"I work for him remember? We're engaged, Katherine."

"Look, I said keep out of it. I don't need your opinion."

Jake took in a deep breath and blew it out in frustration. "Don't you realize you'll never build that hotel if he doesn't want you to? Why don't you build one somewhere else?"

"Thanks a lot. I was hoping you would stick by me. Instead, you side with him. Well I've got news for you. That hotel is going up with or without you. Got it!"

"God, you're impossible sometimes."

"That's the way I am so get used to it or get out while you still can."

The next morning, Cole was up early enjoying another heavenly sunrise. Katherine was due any time.

The peace was broken a few minutes later by the sound of Katherine's helicopter. It landed a short ways from the guesthouse.

Cole ran under the blades and they were in the air in a matter of moments.

"Mornin', cowboy."

Cole adjusted his headset. "Did you see that sunrise?"

"You surprise me being a city boy and all."

"They're spectacular here at the ranch."

After a short flight over the gulf, the island became viewable. They circled the north tip and Katherine pointed out an area they were currently working on.

"The dredge takes sand from the bottom and pumps it to the surface where we need it."

The helicopter landed and the engines shut down.

"We'll be back in a little while, Jimmy." She exited the chopper.

They walked through the sandy ground until they came to the hotel site.

Cole looked excited. "Wow! You've cleared away a lot of brush and debris since I was here last. It's really going to happen isn't it?"

"Yes, it surely is. Can I ask you something kind of personal?"

"Ask away." He looked around at all she had done to the island.

"What are you going to do with yourself now that you sold your company?"

"I really haven't thought about it too much."

Katherine looked at him and held his hand. "Help me build my hotel, Cole. I need someone who believes it can happen. I need your strength to keep me going through this. God only knows the obstacles we'll have to overcome. Please, say yes."

Cole looked into her beautiful and tempting blue eyes, "Katherine, there's nothing else I'd rather do."

22

MARTY'S SMALL BOAT touched the shore of Paradise Island a little after ten p.m. He quickly covered it with some brush and scanned the area to see if he had been spotted. Just like he thought, this was going to be easy.

He walked up to the construction workers quarters and peeked in the windows. He saw a dozen guys playing cards and figured he could go anywhere without being spotted.

He made his way to the construction site and looked for something he could sabotage. "We'll see who can outsmart who, sis'," Marty whispered to himself.

He picked up a gallon of oil and poured it in the fuel tank of the motor supplying power to the island. "That should do for starters. Let's see what else I can do."

The engine sputtered and the perimeter lights flickered on and off. After a couple of minutes, the motor failed and the island went dark. Immediately, a second motor started and the lights came back on.

"Damn, she's got a back up power supply."

Marty saw the door to the construction quarters open and two men walked toward the sabotaged engine to check it out. He hid behind a fuel shack and watched them. But as he stepped back further, something grabbed his legs.

"Oh god, something's attacking me! Help! Help me!" He yelled as loud as he could. He couldn't see what it was because of the darkness. What kind of animal was tugging at his legs? He thought.

The two construction workers ran to the noise and found him hanging upside down from a rope around his feet. They shined their flashlights on him and watched him swing back and forth.

One of them walked toward him. "Well, what do we have here? I think we caught us a varmint, Danny."

Danny laughed. "Yah, I ain't ever seen anything so ugly before."

Marty wasn't in the mood for jokes. "Just get me down from here and make it fast. Do you know who I am?"

"Are you the one who messed with that motor?"

"Look, I'm Katherine's brother and I don't think she would appreciate you keeping me up here like this. Now get me down from here!"

The worker looked up at him. "Tell you what; we'll let Miss Wentworth decide what to do. Danny, go give her a call."

"No don't do that. Just get me down first," Marty pleaded.

Danny ran to the phone and the other man came close to him.

Marty tried to bargain with him. "Look, I'll give you money; just get me down before she comes."

"Too late, she's already here."

Marty saw Katherine and Cole walking toward him with all of the construction crew behind them. How could he let this happen? He thought.

Katherine stopped when she saw him hanging by the rope. "My, my, what have you men caught in your snare?"

One man confessed. "It's my fault, Miss Wentworth. I set a trap for the wild pigs."

Katherine smiled at him. “You should win a trophy, Billy. That’s the biggest wild pig I’ve ever seen.”

All of the men laughed.

Cole looked up at Marty. “So, what brings you to our little island, Marty? Did you have anything to do with the lights going off?”

“I didn’t do shit to your lights. Now would someone please get me down from here?” His face turned red from hanging so long.

Danny held up the cap to the fuel tank. “I think he put something in the fuel. I’ll have to drain the tank.”

Katherine walked around her brother. “Why would you want to do that, Marty?”

Marty lashed back. “I’m getting’ real tired of being on the bad end of your sick jokes. Would you please just lower me down so I won’t pass out?”

Katherine nodded to the men. “Get him down, guys. We wouldn’t want to damage a mind like his.”

Two men lowered Marty and untied the knot around his feet.

Marty brushed himself off and looked at Katherine. “Do you have a thing about hanging people up?”

She gave him a questionable look. “Do you want to tell me why you’re here?”

“I wanted to see how your hotel was coming along.”

Cole came close to him and Marty backed up. “So you screw up our power before you say hello? You’re a terrible liar, Marty.

Katherine crossed her arms. “Does daddy even know you’re here?”

Marty starred at the ground. “No, it was my idea. I’m sick of the way you’re treating dad and me.

She starred at her brother. “Then you’re really not going to like this. Billy, take all of his clothes from him before you put him back in his boat.”

Marty looked shocked. “What! You can’t be serious? I didn’t do anything.”

Cole came close to him. “Don’t show your face on this island again.”

Katherine smiled at him. “Tell everyone I said hello when you get back. Have a nice trip.”

Two men grabbed his arms and walked him toward his boat.

Marty resisted and yelled the whole way. “Wait! Don’t do this, Katherine! I’ll look like a fool!”

23

THE CHARTERED BOAT reached the shore of Paradise Island at nine thirty in the morning. It was already ninety degrees and humid.

The overweight building inspector's shirt was wet with sweat. He wiped the perspiration from the back of his neck with his handkerchief while he got out of the boat.

He was met by two security guards that approached the boat.

One of them questioned his arrival. "How can I help you?"

The inspector held a clipboard in his hand. "I'm looking for Katherine Wentworth."

"May I ask what this regards?"

"Yes, I'm from the building inspecting office from Houston."

The security guard smiled at his partner and talked into his cell phone. "Miss Wentworth, there's a building inspector here that would like to see you. Yes, ma'am." He closed up the phone and talked to his partner. "This should be interesting."

The inspector wiped more sweat from his face when he saw Katherine coming toward them. When she was close, he smiled at her. "Good morning. Are you Katherine Wentworth?"

Katherine was dressed in faded jeans with a light blue top. Her long blond hair was pulled back in a ponytail. She was even stunning to look at with her work cloths on. She looked the inspector over and instantly knew he was not used to this kind of environment. He looked more like a pencil pusher that rarely got out of the office. "Yes, what can I do for you?"

"I'm Robert Mitchell from the department of building services. I'm here to verify your building permits. I'd also like to look at anything you've started on."

She smiled at him and chuckled. "Why would you want to do that?"

The inspector lost his smile. "You have to have permits, Ms. Wentworth or I'll have to shut your operation down."

"Mr. Mitchell, I don't need permits on this island. It's six miles out at sea so none of the laws of Texas apply out here."

He shook his head. "I'm afraid you're wrong there. It clearly states in the building code that if any structure is built within the state it must comply with all laws."

Katherine didn't lose eye contact. "Are you on medication or are you just slow? The key word is within the state of Texas. I just told you this island is six miles off the coast."

The inspector frowned at her. "I don't appreciate being insulted, ma'am, and that could get you in a lot of trouble. I'm a county employee, you know."

"I tell you what, Mr. Mitchell. You get your fat butt back in that boat and get off of my island before I decide to shoot you for trespassing. Is that clear enough for you?"

Both of the security guards smiled at each other.

The inspector looked at her and looked like he was searching for the right words. "Consider yourself officially shut down then." He backed away when Katherine walked toward him.

"If I ever see you here again, I'll make you swim all the way back to Texas," she said.

The inspector climbed back in the boat he arrived in. "You haven't heard the last from me."

Katherine walked closer to the boat. "Mr. Mitchell, I don't know how much my father paid you, but you're lucky you didn't come out of this with at least a black eye. You tell my father he needs to do his homework if he wants to shut my operation down." She turned to one of the security guards. "Danny, shove 'em off. If he shows up again, you have my permission to shoot him."

The security guard shoved the boat away from the shore. "It would be my pleasure, ma'am."

24

COLE SAW THE blue and red lights flashing in his rearview mirror and pulled over to the curb. He had no idea what he had done wrong but got his driver's license out of his wallet.

The police officer got out of his car and came around to the passenger side of Cole's car. "License and registration please."

Cole handed him both.

The officer looked the identification and the car over. “Can I ask you to step out of the car, Mr. Tyler.”

Cole looked puzzled when he said that. “Sure.”

The officer grabbed Cole’s arm. “Put your hands on the roof and spread your feet.”

Cole did as he asked but questioned why. “Can I ask what the problem is, officer.”

He frisked Cole and put handcuffs on him. “Have a seat in my car.” He led him to his back seat and buckled his seat belt when he was inside.

When the officer read him his rights, Cole felt his face flush. “I understand my rights, now what the hell is going on?”

The officer walked to Cole’s car then came back with a baggie full of white powder and held it up. “You want to tell me where you got this.”

Cole couldn’t believe this. “Where did you find that? That’s the first time I’ve seen it.”

The officer looked like he doubted him. “Uh huh, I’ve never heard that before. You can explain it to the detectives because I’m taking you to jail.”

Cole rolled his eyes. “God, I can’t believe this. I have no idea how that got in my car.”

“Tell me something I haven’t heard before. Every single person I arrest for drugs always says the same thing.”

When they arrived at the police station, Cole was booked and fingerprinted.

The detective led him to a small room with no windows and told him to sit. After he removed the handcuffs Cole took off his jacket and the questioning began. "Mr. Tyler, we can help you out of this mess if you can tell us where you purchased the cocaine."

Cole rubbed his hands where they had been handcuffed. He looked at the mirror on the wall and knew other people would be watching from behind it. "I didn't even know it was cocaine that you found. How can I tell you something I don't know anything about?"

The detective chewed his gum too fast. "Do you know what the penalty is for that amount of narcotics in the state of Texas? Twenty years, Mr. Tyler. Now, would you like to sit in the state penitentiary for the next twenty years because you want to protect some drug pusher?"

Cole looked up at the detective. "I've never seen those drugs before and I have no idea why they were in my car."

"Okay, the boys will sure like your sweet little ass when you get to prison. Lock him up." Another detective grabbed Cole's arm and handcuffed him again.

Cole walked down a long, narrow hall to the cellblock. He stopped when the detective turned him over to another police officer.

The officer took him through several locked jail doors until he reached an empty cell. He opened the cell door and shoved Cole in. He took the handcuffs off and threw him an orange jump suit. Then he put rubber gloves on and snapped them. "Give me your clothes and bend over before you put the jump suit on. It's cavity search time for you."

Cole undressed and went through the horrible ordeal of the intense search. All of the other inmates watched from their cells and yelled out disgusting comments. He put the orange jail clothes on when he finished and sat on the small bed when the guard closed the door.

Two hours later, he awoke to footsteps that stopped in front of his cell. He looked up from the small bed and saw Martin Wentworth looking at him under the brim of his dress cowboy hat.

"Hello, Cole."

"Martin, what are you doing here?" Cole stood up and grabbed the bars.

"Maybe I should ask you the same question. You're in a lot of trouble, son."

"How did you even know I was here? I never got my phone call."

"Well that's just unfair treatment. I have a lot of pull with these boys down here. Maybe I could get that phone call for you."

"What did you do, Martin. Wait, you set me up?"

"Lets just say I could make this whole nightmare go away or let it continue for the next twenty years." He smiled at Cole.

"You son of a bitch. Why would you do this to me?"

"I heard through the grapevine that you're helping Katherine build that hotel on her island. Now why would you want to do that?"

Cole stared at him. "Why would you care if I did?"

"I'm afraid that information is confidential. So, here's the deal I'm offering you. I'll have this door unlocked and you can get your life back just like nothing ever happened. Now here's the catch. You leave for California and forget about my daughter and that hotel. Does that sound fair to you?"

"I guess I should have known better than to do business with you."

"You should have gone back to where you came from and stayed out of my business and my state. You're lucky that I like you, Cole. I could make the charges stick and let you sit in prison for twenty years. But I'm giving you another chance and by God you better take it. Oh and Cole, this is the only chance you have. I'll turn you into fish food if I have to deal with you again"

"You don't give me much choice, do you?"

"We all have choices. But sometimes you need a sign to steer you in the right direction. Did I put up a big enough sign for you?"

Martin walked away and the guard unlocked the door.

25

ON SATURDAY MORNING, Governor Simms sipped coffee with Martin, Matt, and Jake in Martin's office at the ranch.

Austin swept for electronic bugs before they started to talk. When he gave the okay, Martin got down to business.

"Okay, gentleman, we have a problem on the island. We need to put our heads together to figure out how we can solve it. We can't have any more incidents like the other day with the helicopter. We looked like idiots, and we're losing a lot of money when our operation isn't operating at full capacity. Any suggestions?"

"Okay I say let's feed her to the sharks," Marty said with alcohol heavy on his breath.

Governor Simms spoke up. "Martin, I'll do what I can to get a court order to stop the construction, but the island is in the gulf. Technically she's not under Texas jurisdiction."

Martin frowned at him. "Dex, I didn't put you in office to hear that. You find a law somewhere or if you can't then make one up. Hell, I don't care what you do. Just use your power to stop that hotel from going up." Martin turned his head. "Jake, I want you to persuade Katherine to let your crew build her hotel. We need to delay it as long as possible."

Jake looked surprised. "I don't know if she'll go for that, Martin."

"That's not a request. You make it happen! Have you forgotten this is your money too? This is serious business, gentlemen, and I expect results. Don't forget we're the ones with the upper hand. My over ambitious daughter has taken on more than she can handle. Now it's time we show her what power is all about." Martin drank from his coffee cup.

Matt broke the short silence in the room. "How far away is the dredging operation from the drop off point?"

"It's completely on the other end of the island." Austin unfolded a map of the island. "About three quarters of a mile or so."

"Let's sabotage the dredge," Matt said.

"She's got twenty guards watching it. It would be almost impossible," Austin said.

Martin looked at the map. "Then let's hit the supply boats going there. She's got to ship everything from the mainland."

"Why don't we just blow the place all to hell?" Marty slumped in a chair across the room.

Martin looked up from reading the map. "As crude as it sounds, that might be another way to go. If she gets a start on this hotel and gets some money into it, we could kill her confidence if we blew the damn thing up. Her investors would have to be complete morons to keep giving her money after that."

The other men nodded in agreement.

Martin sat behind his desk. "Jake, talk her into that contract. With your crew we can easily slow down the pace of that project."

"She's not that stupid, Martin. She'll never give me the job," Jake said.

Martin glared at Jake. "Well, let me put it to you this way. You get that contract or you're through with my company. Every contract you hold with me is gone unless you can talk her into this. So you better brush up on your acting skills and give an academy award performance. Everything you've got is riding on it."

Jake fell back into the chair and just gave a blank stare. When the meeting was over, Jake left the ranch and stopped off at his favorite country western steak house. He drank whiskey with beer chasers and soon was so drunk he couldn't walk.

The bartender knew Jake and called a cab for him. He loaded Jake in it, and sent him home.

Katherine immediately came out when the cab pulled up and she helped Jake in the house.

"What happened?" Katherine had never seen him like that before.

"I love ya', darlin'."

"You look like you've been rode hard and put up wet. Care to tell me what the drunk was all about?"

"Oh, I just drank a little too much at Smitty's." He held his hands over both eyes.

"I see. Don't want to talk about it?"

He managed a smile. "Let's have a candlelight dinner tonight at home. Just the two of us, with romantic music."

"I'd like that, sweetie. Then you can tell me why you drank so much. Okay?"

"Deal. I'll see you tonight then?" He barely had his eyes open.

At seven p.m., they ate a wonderful dinner, and as promised, the candles burned and the music was soft and romantic. Afterward, they kissed on the couch and held each other.

Jake looked into her beautiful blue eyes. "You know I could help you with your hotel."

"What? You wined and dined me and now you want to talk about business?" She sipped her wine.

"I thought about your hotel and what you said to me the other night. I should be more supportive of your project."

"So why the change of heart all of a sudden?" She was suspicious.

"I thought about what you said and I feel bad about it. I want my crew to build your hotel for you."

She snuggled up to him. "Let's not talk about it now. Carry me up to bed and show me how much you love me."

"Okay, but promise me I can build your hotel for you first?"

"Honey, I don't want to spoil the evening by talking about business." She drank the rest of her wine.

"Not until you promise me I can build your hotel." He gulped a whole glass of wine down.

"Hey, you're ruining the mood here, cowboy. Take me to bed before I get out of the mood." She kissed him.

Jake sat up and broke her embrace. He took a long drink from the wine bottle. "Darlin', I want to build that hotel for you and it's important to me to get the contract."

Katherine sat up on the couch. "What's going on, Jake? You always jump at the chance to take me to bed."

"I just need to know if I can help you."

"No, it's a lot more than that. Tell me what's going on."

"First you want me to support you now you don't. I don't know why you won't just tell me if I can build your damn hotel!" He yelled.

"Because I'm not comfortable with you working with my father! That's why you could never build my hotel. He put you up to this didn't he?"

"Why would you think that? I'm my own man and I'm trying to do what's best for both of us."

"You're not your own man when you work for my father. You do what he orders you to do. What did he threaten you with if you don't get the contract?"

He took a deep breath and looked away. "I'll lose every contract I have with Texmar. It will bankrupt my company."

"Tell me why he wants you to get the contract?"

He looked at the ground. "I don't know why."

"Look at me and tell me why he wants you to have the contract!"

"He wants to delay your project as long as possible. There, are you happy now?"

Katherine walked across the room and thought. "As many times as I told you not to do business with him, you wouldn't listen. You have to break free of him, sweetheart, or you'll always be a pawn in his chess game. You're an excellent builder and you can make it without him."

His eyes filled with tears as pleaded with her. "If you don't give me this contract, I'm through."

"That's not the man I fell in love with. You had visions of great projects you were going to build. You can still do those things, honey.

"I'm at the top now, Katherine. How could I start all over again?"

"Just like I'm doing. Don't let my father take your dreams away. He only wants what's best for his company. He'll use you until he doesn't need you any more. Then toss you out like garbage and do the same thing to someone else. I've seen it happen all of my life."

Jake stood up. "Okay, I'll meet you upstairs after I use the bathroom first."

While Katherine walked upstairs, Jake walked into the bathroom, put his pistol in his mouth, and without hesitation pulled the trigger.

26

MARTIN LEFT THE ranch at seven o'clock Monday morning for work and questioned the driver when he entered the limousine. "Where's my normal driver?"

"John is sick today, sir."

"Just step on it, son. I hate being late for work."

"Yes, sir."

Ten minutes went by before Martin realized the limo wasn't going in the direction of the Wentworth building. He picked up the phone and questioned the driver. "Just where the hell do you think your going?"

The driver didn't answer him.

"Hey driver! Stop this car right now!" Martin yelled.

But the driver said nothing and kept the limo moving at a high rate of speed.

Martin reached in his briefcase and pulled out a small pistol. "Pull this damn car over or I'll blow your head off!" He pointed the pistol at the driver. But Martin knew the glass partition, separating him from the driver was bullet proof and the pistol would do nothing.

After ten minutes, the limo turned into a rock quarry. He sped down a dirt road and stopped close to the edge of a gigantic hole where they had taken out a massive amount of rock.

The driver got out and left Martin alone. Then, the back door opened, and two men entered. They took the pistol from him, and sat in the limo seat facing him. The door on the opposite side of Martin opened and another man sat next to him. The well dressed man was in his late fifties to early sixties and had dark brown skin.

"Good morning, Mr. Wentworth." The man spoke with an Italian accent.

"Who the hell are you?" Martin didn't want him to see the real emotions he felt.

"I won't detain you too long, Mr. Wentworth. But I want you to get a good look at the man who is going to kill you." The man smiled at Martin.

"Are you going to tell me who you are or are we going to keep playing games?"

"Very well, my name is Benito Viatsi." He looked for his reaction. "Does that name mean anything to you?"

Martin looked at the two thugs that sat in the seat facing him. "Yeah, it means you're a dope pusher. You're the lowest scum of the Earth. That's what the name means to me."

"I see. And I suppose you are squeaky clean?"

"Hey, don't talk to me about my business. You damn people disgust me. Your business is frying people's brains. You don't have a clue what real business is all about."

"We both want the same outcome though. Isn't money and power what we both really want?"

"I don't really care what you want, Benito. Now how long is this going to take because you're wasting my time with this? Either shoot me or get the hell out of my car. You damn Mafia people are such a pain in the butt."

"No, that would be too easy. I want your life to be miserable. I want you to have to constantly look over your shoulder never knowing when or how I will strike. You killed my son Wentworth and you will die for it!" Benito yelled, with rage in his eyes.

"One thing I can't handle is dealing with a guy who puts off his business. Your son was selling drugs to my boy and had fair warning to back off. When your brother decided to take me on, I killed him too. Can you guess who's next?"

"You think I got where I am today by being stupid? If you want to kill me then stand in line. You could never get to me with all of the guns that protect me." He laughed at Martin.

"Now there you go being stupid again. Those words will come back to bite you in the butt." Martin refused to be intimidated.

"You think this is a game? I could shoot you right here if I wanted."

"What happened to looking over my shoulder? Or you won't know where or when I'll strike. You're about as dumb as they come, Benito. You can't make up your mind on anything, can you?" Martin watched Benito trying to hold his temper.

"Wentworth, I promise you will suffer when you die. We are proud people and our traditions will be honored no matter what you think of us."

"I wish all of you people would get out of my state. You're in my way and I can't wait to get rid of you."

"I'll show you who is in charge in your state. I want you to step out of the car. I will demonstrate to you why you should respect me," Benito said, opening the door and stepping out of the limo.

Martin followed and the two men came out and stood by Benito.

"Okay now what?" Martin looked like he was bored.

Benito's limo was parked about twenty feet away from Martin's limo. The door opened and Martin recognized the woman from Texmar, who sold him newspapers every morning. She had her hands tied and her mouth taped shut. She moaned and cried trying to get away from one of the men.

Benito motioned with his head, and without hesitation, a man threw her into the deep hole.

Martin could hear her faint scream through the gag and then a thud when she hit a few seconds later.

"Does that get your attention? I could have made her suffer, but I'm saving that for you. Think about it every minute of the day, Mr. Wentworth. Look around every corner, because I could be there. My family will have justice for what you did to us. That means no one in your family is safe. So warn them of what will be coming."

"Well I'm shaking in my boots. Are we done now? I've got more important things to do than waste my time here.

Texas will be a lot better off when I put a bullet in your head. You have no idea who you're messin' with," Martin said.

All three of the men got into the limo and sped away.

By the time Martin drove the limo to the Wentworth building, it was past ten a.m. He contacted Austin by phone and let him know what happened.

Austin was in Martin's office when he came up from the private elevator.

"Are you okay, Mr. Wentworth?" Austin asked.

"Yah, Yah. No big deal. Just another pissed off Mafia idiot that wants to kill me. I killed one low life drug dealer, and shit hits the fan. These people don't know when to quit. How many of them do I have to kill?"

"Well that's not all of our troubles," Austin said.

"What's going on?" Martin took off his jacket to change his shirt.

Then, Martin's office door flew open and Matt came in. "Did you hear the latest?" He had a notepad in his hand.

"Will someone tell me what the hell is going on?" Martin was frustrated with them.

"Four of our trucks are missing and the drivers were shot in the head and left in the middle of the road," Matt said.

"What! Tell me none of them were carrying special cargo." Martin got worried.

"One had special cargo," Austin said. "The trucks were hit in California, Texas, Florida, and New York. That means whoever did it is very well connected in every part of the United States."

Matt looked at Martin. "That also means that someone now knows how we make our money."

"Okay, let's not panic. Matt, send every dead driver's family our condolences with a fifty thousand dollar check. I want it to look like the company cares. Austin, lets find out who did this and hit em' back hard. I want a million-dollar contract out on the person responsible. If people out there think we're vulnerable then we'll lose Texmar and I won't have any part of that."

"I heard about the Viatsi thing from Austin. Do you think it's him?" Matt asked.

Martin blew out a breath. "It's a good possibility. He's pretty pissed off at me."

Austin looked at Martin. "Do you think Katherine might be involved in this?"

"She's got nothing to do with this." Martin poured a drink to calm his nerves.

Matt looked worried. "How can you be so sure about that?"

"It's not her style. Trust me, I know my own daughter, and this doesn't have her signature on it." Martin poured a second drink. "Where's Marty anyway?"

"When you didn't come in he left," Austin said.

"I need to warn him about Viatsi. He threatened my whole family and I think he'll probably try something." Martin took another drink of whiskey. "Austin, I want some good men watching my family. I don't want Viatsi picking them off like easy targets."

Austin nodded. "I'll get them posted immediately."

"So what about the cargo, Martin?" Matt asked.

"It's gone and we can't do anything about it. Once we find out who did this, we can handle it." Martin sat behind his desk.

"I'm going to bring you his head, Mr. Wentworth," Austin said, leaving the office.

Martin looked at him. "Do it soon, Austin. We don't have the luxury of time."

"God, I never thought it would come to this." Matt looked devastated.

"Life in the fast lane, big brother. Sometimes it bites back. Don't worry about it. Go back to your office and write those checks to the driver's families. They need our support."

"Martin, we could be indicted for what was on that truck."

"That will never happen. I won't allow it to get out of control. Now let me handle this and give me some time to think."

"Okay, you're right. You always pull us through some how." Matt left Martin's office.

Martin walked to the tall window and looked out at downtown Houston smiling. "Finally, business is getting exciting again."

27

AT FOUR THIRTY, Katherine looked at her watch and wondered where the day had gone. Since Jake's death, she had buried herself in work. She sat in the construction trailer behind her desk when Cole came through the door. She smiled at him when he walked through the office.

Cole sat down in a chair and took his hard-hat off. "It's nice to see you smile again."

"I need a break from this place." She looked at his rolled up shirtsleeves. It exposed his thick forearms and she found herself starring. "Any suggestions?"

"We have a meeting with Garrett and Kyle tonight. What if we meet them back in town and get off of the island awhile?"

"Okay. But only if I can buy dinner tonight after the meeting."

"A beautiful lady invites me to dinner and picks up the tab. How can I turn that down? I'd love to have dinner with you."

"Great! Let's leave right now. I need a break so we can come back and get this place built." Katherine got up to leave.

"All work and no play is no fun." Cole followed her out of the office.

They got in their boat and headed back toward the Texas coast. When they looked back at the island, they saw the structure of steel that was the outline of the hotel. A shared smile told their thoughts without saying a word.

At seven p.m. Katherine entered the Houston hotel where she and Cole were meeting Garrett and Kyle. She was a little early so she went to the lounge for a drink. She noticed two guys at the bar that looked her up and down as she walked by. She took a table toward the back of the room.

The waitress came over to take her order. “If those guys give you any trouble, let me know, and I’ll call security. They’ve been drinking for a couple of hours and gettin’ pretty rowdy. We’ve been looking for a reason to throw them out.”

“Thanks for the warning but I’ll be fine. I’ll have a double whiskey on the rocks.”

The waitress left and one of the guys at the bar staggered over to Katherine.

“Hi there, pretty lady.” He leaned on the table and smelled of alcohol. “I wanna’ buy you a drink.”

“You’re bothering me and I don’t want to drink with you.”

“What, are you too good for me or something?” He slurred his words.

“If you know what’s good for you, cowboy, you’ll go back to your friend at the bar and leave me alone.”

“Well now. We got us a feisty one here, don’t we? You’re pretty when you get mad, darlin’.”

The waitress came back with her drink. “Everything okay here.”

“Yeah, this cowboy was just leaving because if he sticks around, he’ll get hurt.”

"That's it. I'm calling security." The waitress went to the phone.

The guy laughed at Katherine. "You'll like me once you get to know me. I can play rough if that's what you like."

"You know, you've got the manners of a goat. Someone should teach you what no means. Now go back to your friend before you get yourself hurt."

"Well at least dance with me then." He grabbed Katherine by the arm.

"You want to dance?" She got up out of her chair. "Okay, cowboy, let's dance." Katherine took his hand and bent it back until his wrist broke. Then, she kicked him dead center between his legs with her boots and caught the mark perfect.

He went down and his head bounced off of the wooden floor. All six foot two of him lay on the floor out cold.

Security came in one way and Cole, Garrett, and Kyle came in the other, just as the big guy was on his way down. Everyone looked at Katherine in disbelief.

She gulped her whiskey down and walked toward Cole. "He needs to brush up on his manners. Now, let's have that meeting, shall we?"

Cole laughed. "You think I'm going to argue with you after that?"

"Outstanding job, Miss Wentworth," Kyle said.

Garrett looked at security picking the guy up on the floor. “Hey, I’m glad I’m on your side.”

The meeting was in a small meeting room at the hotel.

Kyle placed a black box on the table so their conversation would be private. He began the meeting. “For three months we’ve been investigating why your father has an interest in your island. We’ve spotted several private yachts anchored just off shore. It’s usually early in the morning around one or two. They stay an hour and then take off. This happens three times a week. Then, shortly after the yacht leaves, a small cargo boat stops for about half an hour, then goes to the docks in Houston.”

“So he’s smuggling something?” Cole asked.

“We think he is we just don’t know what it is yet.” Kyle agreed.

Katherine didn’t find it hard to believe. “My father owns a big part of those docks. He can do whatever he wants down there and no one will question it. I’m sure he’s got customs agents on the payroll.”

Kyle took a drink of water. “With his trucks, it would be easy to deliver whatever he is smuggling anywhere he wants. We can keep digging if you want to know what he’s smuggling.”

“Absolutely, I want to know everything,” Katherine said, quickly.

"Okay, whatever you want, Miss Wentworth. I just want to warn you, when you start turning over rocks, you never know what will crawl out," Kyle said.

Katherine smiled. "Thanks for the warning, Kyle, but nothing my father does surprises me. I want to know what the hell he's doing with my island. I'm going to pour a half a billion dollars into a hotel and I don't want any surprises."

"Then we'll start immediately," Kyle said. "That's all I have to report for now."

Cole shook Garrett and Kyle's hand. "Thanks for the great job your doing."

Kyle and Garrett left the room.

Cole looked at Katherine. "Looks like the odds are stacking up against us."

"The odds have been stacked against me all my life, Cole. It's a hurdle, and believe me, we'll overcome it."

"You're confident about it. That's good."

"Nothing will stop me from building this hotel. This is going to be a rough ride so buckle your seat belt. He'll throw everything he's got at us now. We better be prepared to stay on the island for awhile. We'll be safer there."

"I'll start construction on the bungalows so we have a decent place to live."

"Good idea. Maybe in a couple of months we won't feel like we're camping out." Katherine held Cole's hand.

"Thanks for sticking by me on this. You're really special you know." Katherine kissed him on the lips and he kissed her back with more feeling than he had before. "Stay with me tonight," she whispered.

"There's nothing I would like more." He looked deep into her intoxicating, blue eyes.

They left the meeting room and held hands all the way to the car.

The valet brought the car around, Cole handed him a five, and they sped off in Katherine's Jaguar.

Katherine's cell phone rang when they got to the highway and she answered. "Just slow down, Johnnie, now tell me exactly what happened."

Cole looked over at her.

"God no! How bad is it? We'll be there as quick as we can." Katherine hung up the phone and looked at Cole with a horrified look. "There's been an explosion on the island. Johnnie said the steel structure isn't standing anymore. He thinks someone planted explosives and deliberately blew it up. People were killed, Cole."

"Damn. Let's get there as quick as we can and look over the damage." He drove as fast as he could.

Once they docked their boat back on the island, they saw smoke everywhere. The steel structure was torn, twisted, and scattered all over the ground.

Johnnie saw them arrive and ran over to tell them what he knew. The big man was out of breath. "No one saw anything. We just heard an explosion and the structure came crashing down. There's four dead and twelve injured so far."

Katherine looked at her dream hotel in ruins. Then she looked at Cole, "I hate to say it but this is only the beginning. I think things are going to get a lot worse."

28

MARTIN SIPPED HIS drink and read the newspaper in his black limousine. He was surprised when a car bumped them from behind. “Dammit, someone just hit us,” he said to the driver.

When the driver slowed the limo, the car hit them a second time. “I think he’s hitting us on purpose, sir.”

Martin rolled his eyes. “Really, John, what was your first clue? Step on it and lose this guy.”

The limo driver floored it and brought them up to eighty miles an hour on the two-lane country road.

The car that followed sped up and hit them from the left side.

Martin threw his paper down. "You're gonna' have to go faster than that if we're going to lose these guys." He pulled out his cell phone and dialed. "Austin, some asshole is chasing my limousine on Hillerman Road a couple of miles from the ranch. He's hit us three times and is still coming. Get out here and take this guy out."

Austin spoke back. "I'll get there as soon as I can, sir. I'm twenty miles away though."

"Then you better sprout wings because it's probably Viatsi's bunch."

"On my way."

Martin put his phone away. "Wouldn't you know my protection is twenty miles away?"

The car slammed into the left side again and caused the limousine to swerve. When it hit again the limo couldn't stay on the road.

"I can't hold it, sir!" The driver shouted.

Martin's limousine left the road and came to a sudden stop in a field. Its tires sank in the wet mud.

Two men got out of the other car and ran toward Martin. They opened the back door and found him holding a handkerchief on a bloody wound on his head. They both drug him from the back seat and put him on the ground. Then, they put the driver next to him.

Martin tried to catch his breath. “What are you going to do, shoot us?”

The driver whimpered. “I’ve got a wife and two children. Please don’t kill me!”

One of the men pulled out a pistol and put it to the back of the driver’s head.

Martin heard the pop from the gun and figured his life was over too.

The man put the pistol to the back of Martin’s head and clicked the hammer down.

Martin jumped when he heard it but opened his eyes when he heard the two men laughing.

The man with the gun spoke to him. “The Viatsi family says hello. Benito thought this would be too quick of a death for you. He wants time to think about how you will die.”

The two men ran to their car and drove away.

Martin crawled through the mud over to his dead driver, and watched Austin screech his car to a stop.

Austin ran to him. “Thank god you’re okay.”

"Does it look like I'm okay, Austin? I sure don't feel okay. Sons of bitches killed my driver. I won't stand for this kind of behavior. Benito Viatsi has got to go."

29

IT WAS NINETY five degrees in the shade where Marty parked, and he was sweating like a pig in his Porsche. He waited for Cole to appear outside his house.

The door to the house opened and Cole appeared with two suitcases.

Marty opened his door and walked toward him.

Cole saw Marty approach and put the suitcases in his car.

Marty grinned and produced a thirty-eight-caliber revolver. “Going somewhere, Mr. Tyler?”

“Get that gun out of my face.” Cole was irritated that Marty would point a gun at him.

“Sorry to wreck your plans, but you’re coming with me. My father would like a word with you and I’m going to deliver you to him.”

“I said get that damn gun out of my face, Marty!”

“Get your ass in that car and drive!”

“Does your father even know you’re here?”

Marty laughed. “Hey, I’ve got the gun and I’ll ask the questions. Never mind what my father knows, just get in that car before I blow your head off!”

“I’m going to tell you one more time. Get that gun out of my face.”

“This gun will blow a good size hole in you, Tyler. Now get in that car and drive before I have to shoot you.”

Kyle appeared behind Marty, and before Marty knew what happened, the gun was on the ground. Kyle punched him in the face and Marty was out cold. Kyle bound his hands and feet and gagged him.

Cole decided it was time to talk with Martin face to face. He needed to look the enemy in the eye before the war began. He dialed Martin’s private number and arranged to meet him.

Thirty minutes later, Martin Wentworth pulled the new Rolls Royce Corniche up to the curb. “Hop in.”

Cole got in and inhaled the smell of the new leather seats. The burl wood dash surrounded the high tech instrument panel. The signature crystal flower vases were perched high on both sides of the back seats. In another circumstance, the experience would have been nice, but he was there with Martin.

“So, what’s on your mind?”

Cole looked over at Martin. “It’s time we got a few things straight.”

“Well, I’m all ears.” Martin put the car in motion and drove the streets of downtown Houston.

“I know you’re a man that likes to get right down to business. So, I won’t waste any time. There has got to be a good reason why you don’t want Katherine to build the hotel on the island? You want to tell me why?”

Martin smiled. “Let’s just say you’re carrying a big bucket of shit up a steep mountain. And if you’re not careful, you’ll spill it all over you.”

“I’m not here for riddles. Just tell me the reason.”

“When I bought you out, I thought you would start another business in California. That would have been the smart thing to do you know.”

"Katherine is going to build that hotel, whether I help her or not," Cole said. "She's determined to go to war with you if she has to. She won't have it any other way."

Martin laughed. "I know how tough my daughter appears to be. Believe me, she has the heart of a prizefighter. But when the dust settles after this battle, I guarantee there won't be a hotel standing on that island." Martin took his eyes off of the road for a second and locked them with Cole's. "I won't have it any other way."

Cole thought for a moment. "I don't know what you're doing over there, but if it causes you to take this kind of action against your own daughter, I hope it's worth it."

"You know, I'm glad we're having this little chat. I'm going to give you one more chance to leave this state. I have a bag in the trunk with one million dollars cash in it. You can drive it to California in this brand new Rolls Royce. But If I ever see your face in my state again, you're a dead man. That clear enough for you?"

Cole stared at Martin. "I'm sure you could bribe most people with that kind of money. But I wouldn't quit this hotel project if you gave me everything you had."

"This is a one time offer and I advise you to pack your bags and get out while you still can. I'd hate to see you get hurt over this. You should really learn to mind your own damn business."

"I don't scare that easy."

Martin took his eyes off the road shortly. "You know what your problem is, Cole? You just don't know how to take a warning. I'll destroy that hotel if you build it ten times. Or for that matter, I might just kill both of you."

"Only a desperate man would sacrifice his daughter for a business deal."

"I'm also sacrificing my son." Martin looked over for his reaction.

"What does Marty have to do with this?"

"I mean you, Cole."

Cole starred at him with disbelief. "What kind of bullshit are you feeding me now?"

"Do you think I picked your company to buy just out of the blue? I had my reasons for wanting your company."

"Martin, you can't possibly think I believe this."

"Your mother, Claire, was the love of my life in my younger days. When she got pregnant her parents just moved away one day and never came back. I didn't know what happened to you or her until I had a private investigator locate you."

Cole shook his head. "My real father died in Vietnam. I'll give you credit for one thing though, Martin. That's got to be the most creative story I've ever heard why I shouldn't sleep with your daughter. I've had enough of this. Pull over and let me out."

"Well, it's obvious you won't take a warning." Martin changed his tone. "If you take Katherine's side, we'll be enemies. Trust me, you don't want me as your enemy." He drove the car to the curb and stopped.

Cole got out and closed the door. He came down to the open window and looked in at Martin. "I'm building that hotel with Katherine and nothing you do can stop us."

Martin glared at Cole. "Well then, welcome to the war, son."

30

COLE AND KATHERINE sat high on a hill, on Paradise Island, watching the sky being painted with a salmon-colored sunset. From the South, they saw miles of ocean, and from the North, they saw the coastline of Texas.

A breeze blew warm air that mixed with the smell of the ocean. The constant crash of the waves sounded like a hypnotic symphony. As the sky slowly became darker blue, they saw the lights of their supply ship approaching the island.

Katherine stood up. "There it is our new beginning."

Cole saw the ship. "We should have it off loaded by early morning. Then we can go to work again."

Katherine hugged him. "I'm sorry for putting you through all of this, Cole."

"Hey, we're a team, remember? We're going to build this hotel no matter what happens. I knew it wasn't going to be easy."

"Yah, but I bet you didn't know my father was going to be such an obstacle."

"I'll be honest, I didn't think he would be so ruthless, but I'm learning quickly."

Katherine saw Cole smile at the anticipation their new shipment and it brightened her mood. "I hope the added security lets us work without any more trouble."

Cole watched the ship get closer. "We can't let our guard down. Martin won't give up trying to sabotage this hotel."

Katherine found she couldn't look away from Cole. She thought about the way he made her feel and the hope he offered for her future. He made her life new and exciting again. "I've thought a lot about the plans we had the night of the explosion."

"Yeah, me too." He looked at the ground like he was disappointed. "I didn't know if it might have been too soon after you lost Jake."

“I wouldn’t have suggested it if it was.”

“I’ve never felt like this around anyone before, Katherine.” He looked into her seductive, blue eyes and kissed her on the lips.

“You sure know how to charm a girl, cowboy.”

Cole’s cell phone rang. “How could someone interrupt such a perfect moment?” He punched the talk button. “Cole Tyler.”

Katherine watched him put his hand on top of his head. She knew something was wrong.

Cole looked out at the ship closely. “How reliable is the information?” He looked at Katherine and shook his head. “I can’t believe this is happening. I’ll call the boat captain and let him know.”

“What’s wrong?”

Cole ended the connection and dialed seven numbers. “More trouble.” He spoke into the phone. Captain Williams, this is Cole Tyler. I’ve just received some disturbing information about a bomb about to explode on your ship. My source thinks the information is reliable enough for you to abandon ship immediately. I realize this is your decision, sir. I’m only relaying the information I have just received." Cole hung up and looked at the ship.

“He’s done it again! Damn you, daddy!” Katherine yelled.

Then, suddenly the ship exploded, and a wall of fire shot up in the air. The concussion hit the island with such a powerful force that it knocked Katherine and Cole to the ground.

Katherine got up and tears poured out of her eyes. “No! Not again! He can’t do this, Cole!” She shouted.

He held her weak body up after she almost fainted. Cole watched the ship burning a hundred yards from the shore. It lit up the island with thirty-foot high flames. “My God, all those men just died.”

31

AT THREE O'CLOCK in the afternoon, Katherine drove her Jaguar up to a set of tall metal gates and spoke into the intercom. The ten-foot gates opened and she drove up the long driveway.

Tall oak tees shaded the circular drive that lead up to the house and dotted the many acres that spilled off behind it. The lawns were perfectly manicured and multi-colored flowers hugged the edges of the walks. Ten-foot walls made the estate as secure as a fortress. Armed men guarded the

Old Spanish hacienda that had been completely restored to its original beauty. They watched her carefully while one of them opened her car door.

She walked toward the beautiful hand carved, double doors that led to the entrance to Benito Viatsi's home. Katherine rang the doorbell and a butler appeared.

"Good afternoon, Miss Wentworth. Welcome to the Viatsi estate. Please come in, and you can leave the pistol you have in your purse with me. I will see that you get it back when you depart." He held his hand out.

Katherine wondered how he knew she had it. She handed him the pistol and he motioned to follow him.

"Please follow me this way and Mr. Viatsi will see you."

Katherine looked at the way the huge house was decorated and instantly knew that it needed a woman's touch. However, she was not here to give advice on decorating or insult anyone.

After a short walk down a wide hallway, they came to a library with sixteen-foot ceilings. Thousands of books surrounded the room in oak shelves that stretched up the tall walls.

Benito got up from his chair when she entered the room and greeted her. "Miss Wentworth, I am Benito Viatsi, and it is a pleasure to finally meet you." He kissed the back of her hand spoke like an Italian gentleman. He was dressed in an expensive suit and was better looking than she had imagined. "Please sit down. May I offer you a drink?"

"Okay, I'll have a whiskey on the rocks." Katherine sat in the chair next to Benito.

He waved to a servant in a white uniform, and the drinks were served. The doors to the library closed, and Benito and Katherine were alone in the room.

Katherine looked into his dark brown eyes. "You have a beautiful home. It's very charming."

"Thank you. I believe your home should reflect a part of you. I found this Old Spanish hacienda a few years ago and gave it the care it so desperately deserved."

"Well, you've really done a great job and kept everything originally Spanish." Katherine looked around the room.

"I understand you brought your pistol with you today, Miss Wentworth. Did you think there would be trouble?"

"It's only for my protection so please don't be insulted."

"A man like me has to be extra careful. You understand don't you?"

"Of course I do." Katherine took a sip of her drink and mentally prepared herself.

"I must say, Miss Wentworth, I am surprised you're here. Your father and I have had some trouble recently and I think it is very brave of you to show up here today."

"Mr. Viatsi..."

"Please call me, Benito, and may I call you, Katherine?"

"Yes, please do." She smiled at him. "Benito, I want you to know, what my father does has nothing to do with me. I'm feuding with him also."

"I know about the trouble between you and your father. It's my business to know although it's hard for me to understand. In my world, Katherine, my strength comes from our strong family bond."

"I envy your family, and I only wish my father had the values that hold your family together. I would rather work with him instead of fighting over this hotel. However, you and I both know that will never happen."

"Why do you come to me, Katherine? What can I possibly do to help you?"

Katherine stood up from her chair and walked over to the window. She took a stiff drink and a deep breath. "Benito, I'm going to lay my cards on the table. I know you are a man of honor, and no matter what the outcome here is today, I trust you will keep what I say between us."

"You trust me even though I have made threats against your own family?"

"Blood is thicker than water, and if a war ever came between us, we would both fight with our own families. But this is not about family honor. This is about business, Benito, and I know you're a smart businessman."

He studied her for a moment. "You impress me, Katherine, and you are very different from your father. You have strong dedication and you have courage. But I still don't know why you came here today."

"I lost my primary investors in my hotel. We had an explosion that wiped out all of the work I had started." She took a drink of her whiskey and Benito refilled both glasses.

"I'm sure my father had everything to do with it. The point is it's a battle I'll never win alone. He has unlimited resources to fight me with. If I start the hotel again, he'll do the same thing. If my hotel is going to get built, I need your help, Benito."

It was silent for a few moments. "I suppose you will make it worth my trouble?"

Katherine felt like he was interested. "Here's what I propose. I borrow two hundred million from you for the hotel. I will build the hotel and you provide protection. When we open, I'll guarantee you fifty million a year for six years on the two hundred million you put up. That's fifty-percent interest to you on the building money in six years. We split the profits down the middle from day one."

"Sounds like you have it all worked out. You want me to be your partner as well as your protector?"

"Yes, and it's a good deal for both of us, Benito."

"I will need a lot of men to supply protection because your father has a small army himself. I will put up the two hundred million, but only if you let me buy out your interest at the end of one year."

"What! You want my hotel? No way."

"Your hotel will be built with my money, and after you build this hotel, Katherine, you can start another project somewhere else. Besides, this way you don't have to pay me back. I would feel better about my hotel being protected instead of protection for your hotel."

"That makes it your hotel on my island. Why would I even put it up if I don't make anything on it?"

"I will pay you a hundred million to build it and start it up. You still own the island and I will pay you one million a month for leasing it. However, a permanent lease will have to be written up. The hotel is no good to me if you want your island back. That deal makes more sense to me."

"That's a high price to pay for protection."

"You have to make it worth my while, and you must understand, my two hundred million is at serious risk. I will only settle for full ownership after one year."

"I didn't come here to give my hotel to you."

"Yes, but it won't be built unless you have my money and my protection from your father. You will have no hotel, and we both know you won't settle for that."

"Damn you, Benito. You want too much from me."

"You also ask a great deal from me. Who else can provide the kind of protection I can give? I am at risk, can't you see that?"

Katherine tried to keep her cool. "You're getting a gold mine for your trouble. That hotel will make a fortune."

"The price is high for my protection, and what I am protecting is my two hundred million. In my business, I can make even more money quicker than what you offer me. Take it or leave it, Katherine."

She looked out the window. "This thing you have against my family bothers me. If I agree, can you guarantee the threat against my family will go away?"

"I give you my word of honor I will harm no one in your family with the exception of your father. If I provide you protection, I must be able to take him out if he becomes a problem."

"Okay, how you deal with my father is your business, but if anyone else in my family dies mysteriously in the meantime, this deal is terminated, Benito." She shook his hand.

"My attorneys will draw up the documents and construction on the hotel can resume immediately. I assure you Miss Wentworth, the deal we just made will stop your father."

"I guess I should be happy. But why do I feel like I just made a deal with the devil?"

32

AT THE HELIPORT, the porter loaded Cole's luggage into Katherine's helicopter. Cole boarded the helicopter and put the headset on to talk with, Jimmy, the pilot. The helicopter took off before Cole could sit down. He almost lost his balance. "Hey, fly boy. What's your hurry?"

But no answer came through the headset. He regained his balance and walked to the cockpit. He was shocked for a second, and then laughed at what he saw.

The pilot wore dark sunglasses. "Hello, Cole, surprise, surprise."

"Justin! You scared the hell out of me. What are you doing here?"

"We need to talk and I thought this would be a good place. Just you me and the birds up here."

Cole took a seat in the co-pilot's chair. "You pop up in the strangest places."

"Yeah, it's a bad habit I have."

"Since your here there's something I'm puzzled about. You warned us about the supply ship, why didn't you warn us about the explosion we had on the island?"

"I knew I would hear about that. That one slipped by me or I would have. Sorry Cole, this isn't an exact science."

"Well, we may not survive because our investors backed out. We have no money to start building again even if we wanted to."

"That's what I want to talk to you about. The good news is you have operating capitol again. Two hundred million dollars to be exact. You also have protection now against my father."

Cole looked surprised. "I know there's more so I'll hold the questions until you finish."

Justin continued flying the helicopter in over the gulf headed towards Paradise Island. "My sister has been busy making sure this hotel goes up. When that woman gets an idea in her head, she won't quit."

"I've never met anyone quite like her. I guess I shouldn't be surprised." Cole looked down at the water and put on his sunglasses to avoid the intense glare.

"Yeah, she's quite a lady. But there's a down side to this, Cole, and that's what I want to talk to you about."

"I was afraid of that. Good news is in short supply now days."

"You're not going to like your new partner." Justin made another turn going directly to the island.

Cole looked at him. "Who did she get the money from?"

"First, let me tell you this man is a bitter enemy of my father and that could actually be a real advantage. His name is Benito Viatsi."

"The gangster, Benito Viatsi? What the hell got into Katherine?"

"It's the only way she could save the hotel. Look what you're up against. My father has unlimited resources and he doesn't want the hotel to materialize. Katherine can't fight my father and win by herself. He could blow the thing up a hundred times if he wanted to. Benito Viatsi is one of the few men who have the power to stop him. My father fears Viatsi because of his mob connections.

"What does Viatsi get out of all of this? I know he's not doing it for nothing."

"He gets everything, Cole. He gives Katherine two hundred million to build the hotel but she doesn't pay him back. Benito buys her interest in the hotel after a year for one hundred million plus leases the island from her for good."

"How do you think your father will react when he finds out Viatsi is Katherine's new partner?"

Justin made a sharp turn toward the island. "He'll be furious. What I want to convince you of today is Katherine had no other choice. If this hotel is going to be built, then Viatsi had to be brought in as a partner. I'm sure Katherine dreads telling you about this."

Cole studied the water for a minute. "I can't believe it came to this. Katherine had such a good idea and now it's shot down before we can get it off the ground."

"Welcome to the world of the Wentworth's. It's important that she builds the hotel, because if she pulls it off, it proves she can beat my father at his own game. Very few people have ever done that before."

"The more I'm around your family, Justin, the more I realize why you left. This competition thing between Katherine and your father is way out of control."

"Tell me about it. I've lived with it most of my life and you can never escape. I knew if I wanted to live my life the way I wanted I had to leave my family and start again on my own. My father thinks everything he does should go unquestioned. I can't live like that and that's why I'm here with you today."

Cole shook his head. "Well, I'm not happy about the way things turned out. Benito Viatsi is going to be trouble. He'll bring in his drug money to build the hotel and that will attract the Fed's attention."

"They won't find out about it until Katherine sells him the hotel. You'll be long gone from the deal when the Fed's know anything about it. Viatsi is smart enough to keep this deal quiet until he takes over."

"So Katherine builds the hotel, gets a hundred million dollar profit and then what?"

"You'll have to ask her that question. She's waiting for you on the island."

"I really wanted to run that hotel with her. Now, it will never happen."

"I guarantee if you hang around with Katherine very long, you'll have a lot of opportunities. She would have been bored with it after a year or so anyway."

The helicopter landed on the island, and Cole unbuckled his seatbelt.

"One thing before I go, Justin. Your father told me something today that bothered me."

"I know what it is, and it came as a surprise to me too. If he is your real father it would make us half brothers, you know."

"It would also make Katherine my half sister."

"Yah, I know." Justin rubbed his chin.

"Find out anything you can. I have to be sure about this before I get involved with her."

"Okay, I'll look into it."

Cole looked him straight in the eye. "Justin, it's important I know the truth."

"Go cheer up my sister."

Cole opened the door and got his bags.

Justin gave him the thumbs up sign and took off.

Katherine was standing nearby waiting for him.

Cole walked toward her and the very sight of her made him feel good.

The two of them hugged while she cried.

Cole wiped her tears. "Hey, what's all the crying for?"

"We have to talk." She took the handkerchief that Cole handed her.

"Katherine, what ever it is, we'll get through it."

33

KATHERINE'S HAIR BLEW in the strong wind as she came in the construction office. When she closed the door, the papers pinned to the corkboards slowly floated back down.

The construction superintendent walked over to her. "Mornin', Miss Wentworth. I hate to spoil your day so early, but we're receiving some disturbing weather reports. A hurricane warning came in about an hour ago. If it continues on its present course, we'll get hit."

Katherine rubbed her temples. “Great, that’s all we need right now. I thought the wind was blowing really hard today.”

Cole came in the door and went straight for the coffee. “Good morning, everyone. The wind sure is blowing a lot of sand around.” He poured him and Katherine a cup. He put cream and sugar in hers and handed it to her. “From the looks of both of you I must have missed something.”

“Johnnie just told me a hurricane is headed straight for us.”

Cole’s smile left his face. “Are you serious?”

Johnnie walked back from the computer with a printout of a satellite weather picture. “I’m afraid so. Here’s the latest shot and it looks like we’re gonna’ get slammed real hard.”

Cole and Katherine studied the map and saw the swirl of clouds spinning toward the Gulf of Mexico.

Johnnie gave them some hope. “There’s always a possibility it could change course. Trying to predict Mother Nature is impossible, but we need to prepare for the worst. Even if it got close, it could wipe out everything we’ve started.”

Cole looked at the superintendent. “What can we do to get ready for it, John?”

He looked down at the floor then at Cole. “I’m afraid there’s not much we can do, Mr. Tyler. We’re sitting ducks out here because we don’t have anywhere to go. These temporary trailers we live and work in will blow away like matchsticks. How do you prepare for that?”

The wind picked up speed and rocked the construction trailer. They all looked at each other.

Katherine knew the workers were her responsibility. They had nowhere to go to get shelter from the storm. She realized now, her oversight could cost all of them dearly. “The first thing I should have done is had you dig the shelters. My god, this could be a catastrophe.”

The wind blew harder and rocked the construction trailer again. The windows whistled with the strong gusts.

Johnnie put on his hardhat and walked to the door. “It’s getting worse. I better get the crew to tie down everything we can.”

Cole watched Katherine worry. “Hey, don’t go blaming yourself for this. There’s no way you could have known a storm like this would hit so soon.”

She wiped a tear and looked out the window. “No more should have to die for this hotel, Cole. These men all have families.”

The fierce wind tilted the office and the force got even stronger.

Cole looked out the window. Debris blew over the entire island. "Well, we can't stay here that's for sure."

Something hit the construction trailer hard and put a hole in the wall two feet wide. The wind rushed in and several papers flew around the office.

Katherine held on to Cole's arm and yelled to him over the noise. "Where do we go?"

Cole grabbed her hand. "Let's get to the mountain. Maybe there's someplace we can all find cover." He opened the door and the powerful wind snapped it off the hinges.

They jumped three-foot down because the steps had blown over. The intense wind filled the air with blowing sand and debris. They shielded their eyes with their hands and could barely see where they were going.

Suddenly, a large piece of metal hit Cole and he went down.

Katherine screamed when she saw him bleeding from his chest. "Cole! Oh god no! Cole! Someone please help!"

Cole moaned in pain on the ground as Katherine yelled to anyone that could hear. But the intense wind made it impossible to see anyone or hear anything.

Katherine kept screaming desperately for help. She felt Cole's hands touch her face and tried to focus her eyes. Why did her surroundings suddenly look different? Why couldn't she hear the wind and see all of the debris in the air anymore?

Cole shook her. “Katherine, wake up. Come on, you’re having a nightmare.”

Katherine looked into Cole’s eyes and tried to accept what was happening. “Cole, you’re all right.” She hugged him.

“I heard you yelling from next door. Are you okay?”

She wiped the tears from her face with a tissue he handed her. “We have to build storm shelters immediately. It’s a matter of life and death.”

34

MARTIN WALKED OUT the front door of his home and realized he didn't say good bye to his wife, Amanda yet. He walked back inside, gave her a big hug, and kissed her.

"I thought you might have forgotten about me." She smiled at him.

"How could I forget about the prettiest lady in Texas?"

"You always did know how to charm me. Have a good trip, dear. I'll see you Wednesday for our dinner party."

"I'll be there and I know it will be the talk of the town, darlin'." Martin walked out of the large home and got into the limousine.

Five minutes later, his cell phone rang. "Good morning, Mr. Wentworth." The man spoke with an Italian accent.

"How did you get this number, Viatsi? This is my private line and I don't allow worms like you on it."

"Such harsh words on this beautiful day."

"What the hell do you want? I've got no time for you."

"I just want you to be careful on your business trip. You never know when that jet of yours might blow up or an engine might stall. Accidents often happen without much warning."

"Am I supposed to be afraid now?" Martin took a big drink of whiskey.

"I don't suppose anything would scare a powerful man like you. Oh, by the way, I want to warn you to keep away from Paradise Island. I'm Katherine's new partner and I will be protecting my new investment rather carefully."

"What! You keep your damn drug money away from my daughter."

"I'm afraid it's too late for that. You see, she came to me because she knew I could stop you from destroying her hotel."

"You stay away from my daughter and that island or you're a dead man!

"I knew you would be pleased when you heard I was her new partner. I wanted to give you the good news myself. Have a nice trip."

The line went dead and Martin threw the phone down.

The limo arrived at the airport and Martin got out at his private hanger. He walked quickly towards his jet and found his mechanic making the final maintenance checks.

"How well did you check her out, Denny?" Martin looked at him under the brim of his dress cowboy hat.

"I did a complete system check and looked for anything unusual, Mr. Wentworth."

"Well, do it again, because I have reason to believe something might be wrong. Be thorough and don't miss an inch because it's my ass if you do."

"Okay, Mr. Wentworth, I'll check her out again, but it'll take an hour."

"Okay, let me know when you're done. I'll be inside catching up on some work."

After an hour of an intense search, the mechanic still didn't find anything unusual. He boarded the jet and saw Martin at work on a laptop computer.

"She's as clean as a whistle, Mr. Wentworth."

"Okay, Denny." Martin handed him a hundred-dollar bill. "Thanks for your trouble."

"Thank you, Mr. Wentworth, anytime." He smiled at the generous reward. He came down from the jet and grabbed a rag to wipe his hands.

Martin dialed the phone and Austin immediately answered.

"Yes, sir."

"Austin, the jet checked out and I'm headed for Corpus Christi. Keep an eye on drug boy for us. I think he's bluffing about the jet."

"Are you sure you want to take a chance on it? You know how sneaky he is."

"I had Denny check it out twice and he said it's clean. Besides, I've got to get to Corpus Christi for a business meeting. Viatsi isn't going to scare me that easy."

"It's your call, Mr. Wentworth. I don't trust Viatsi, and I'm uncomfortable about the jet."

"You should be, Austin. Hell, that's what I pay you for. Listen, I'll call you when I get there. I want to know every move Viatsi makes so watch him close."

"Yes sir, I've already got him wired for picture and sound. If he goes to the bathroom, I'll have it on tape."

"Gee, there's a pretty thought. Call me if anything develops." Martin hung up the phone and punched the numbers to place a call to the pilot.

"Yes, sir." The pilot answered.

"Yah, Billy, Denny is done checking her out so we can get on to Corpus Christi now. Listen, I've got a ton of work to catch up on so don't disturb me unless you have to. Okay, partner?"

"Yes, sir. I'll take her up easy so you won't be disturbed. I'll let you know when we're fifteen minutes from touchdown."

"Appreciate it, Billy." Martin thought about the phone call he got earlier from Viatsi.

The jet quickly got up to speed and took off.

Martin looked at the light blue sky and his thoughts changed from business to his family.

Martin knew he was lucky to be married to Amanda. A lot of women would have left years ago because it wasn't easy being married to Martin Wentworth.

He had his hands full with Katherine. She had proven to be extremely persistent and an unexpected and clever adversary.

Then there was his oldest son, Justin, who left because they fought bitterly about Texmar. He missed him and wondered what ever became of him.

He thought about his youngest daughter, Tiffany, and how beautiful she was. She would be like her mother, and become a sophisticated, Southern lady.

He thought about his son, Marty, who was trying, but didn't seem to have the brains to run Texmar. He worried about Marty and his future.

Cole and Katherine watched the news anchor on television and could hardly believe what they were hearing.

"This breaking news just in. At seven p.m. this evening the private company jet owned by Houston based Texmar Corporation suddenly exploded over the Gulf of Mexico. The jet was believed to be carrying Texmar founder Martin Wentworth along with his pilot, William Henderson. Witnesses who saw the explosion said it was a spectacular fireball that lit up the evening sky followed by showers of fiery debris falling into the Gulf of Mexico."

35

THE MOTORCADE LEADING the long procession of limousines could be heard a mile away before it arrived at the Southern Star Ranch. Six double rows of police motorcycles rolled through the massive ranch gate. They were followed by six black Chevy Suburbans with dark tinted windows. They escorted eight black limousines all flying the American flag. One limousine in the middle of the group flew the flag of the President of the United States. Four more black Suburbans followed the limousines.

Before the motorcade arrived, the Secret Service had already combed the Southern Star Ranch for hours. Several agents got out when they came to a stop.

The limousines sat on the dirt road close to the burial site for another five minutes.

The doors finally opened and President Claborne came out dressed in a black suit. He walked toward Amanda Wentworth and gave her his condolences.

The First Lady got out of another limousine and hugged Amanda.

The Wentworth family was lined up and greeted the President and First Lady after Amanda had a moment with them.

Matthew introduced his wife and children to the President and First Lady.

Then Katherine introduced Cole to them.

Marty didn't know what to do and just seemed awkward with the whole situation.

Tiffany got a hug from the First Lady and the President commented on how tall that she had gotten since the last time he had seen her.

A Secret Service agent then escorted the first family to their seats and told them the service would begin soon.

There were over five hundred people at the funeral.

Several executives from Texmar attended not knowing the fate of the company or the status of their jobs.

All of the biggest people in national and state politics and business attended.

Secret Service agents surrounded the chairs and formed a defense perimeter. All of them wore dark sunglasses and had earpieces in their ears.

News networks covered the funeral and the vans were lined up a few hundred yards away. Their satellite dishes were ready to feed the funeral footage to millions of people.

The wind blew softly from the East and the leaves on the hundred year old oak trees hummed on the trees. It smelled of dried grass mixed with floral scents from the hundreds of flowers that surrounded the chairs. The wind was a welcome relief because some of the people were not covered by the white overhead canvas tarps.

The funeral lasted forty-five minutes and the highlight was when the President of the United States gave the eulogy. He painted the picture of a man who should be remembered for the many good things he left us with and the generous ways he gave back to society. Although there were several people there that knew Martin wasn't like that, coming from the mouth of the President of the United States, it was believable.

When the funeral was over several people came up to give their condolences to the Wentworth family and that lasted for about an hour.

The President had gone to the main house and used Martin's office at Amanda's insistence.

When Katherine and Cole arrived at the main house a Secret Service agent told Katherine that the President requested to speak with her in private.

When Katherine got to her father's office, two agents guarded the door.

"One moment, ma'am," One of them said, as he went inside and closed the door. He returned in a matter of seconds and said, "The President will see you now, ma'am." He opened the door for her.

Katherine came into the office and President Claborne talked on a secure phone at her father's desk. He smiled at her when she entered the room.

One of the Presidents aides offered her a drink and she took a whiskey on the rocks. When she got her drink the President hung up the phone, stood up, and hugged her.

"Hello Katherine. You look as beautiful as always." He flashed his charismatic smile. "I hope you don't mind if I take a few minutes of your time. I know this is a rough time for you but I don't get a chance to see you as often as I would like."

"I always have time for you, Gordon. What's on your mind?" She took a drink of her whiskey.

"This isn't the best time to bring this up but I have to work things in as I can."

She was curious. "I appreciate your concern but I didn't exactly have a close relationship with my father. Say what you have to say."

"God I love you Texas women. I wish I had half the backbone that you have. Bob, pour me a whiskey would you? I'd like to have a drink with this young lady."

The aide brought the drink to him immediately.

He touched his glass to hers and they both drank.

"What's on your mind?" Katherine kept her poker face.

"I was talking to Conner Whitman, chairman of the Texas Republican Party, a few weeks ago and he informed me that Senator Newland will not be seeking reelection. He seemed to think that you would be an outstanding choice to fill his seat and I agreed."

"Come on, Gordon. You know that I have no political ambition."

"I know that, Katherine but I'd like you to at least consider it. You would have my full support and I'll even speak at some of your rallies. It won't hurt you to toss it around a little."

"Okay, I won't dismiss it entirely, but why me? There has to be a hundred other good candidates."

"Believe me, you have a quality about you that isn't found in too many people. I've sparred with the best of them and I know how tough you are. I'm asking the person who I think could do the best job."

"You flatter me but I'm in the middle of a project right now and I'm way too busy to take anything on like that." She sipped her drink.

"I know about the hotel and I also know that in a year you'll be done with it. Senator Newland has two more years in office and you could prepare for the election the year after your hotel is built. You have time to finish your hotel and run for the Senate afterwards."

"You are the salesman, aren't you?" She knew he had rehearsed this speech.

"It's my duty to get the right person for the job." He shot her another smile.

"I'll consider it but won't promise anything."

"See there, you already passed the first test. A politician never promises anything."

An aide came over to him and whispered something in his ear.

"I wish I had more time but duty calls." He stood up, came from around the desk, and gave Katherine a big hug.

"Thanks for coming, Gordon. I know my father would have been proud to know that you came."

"Your father helped me get to where I am today. I would like to return the favor any way I can." He turned and started to walk towards the door and before he got there turned backed to her. "You know, Katherine, many other opportunities could open up for you in politics. A woman as strong as you could wind up President of the United States one day."

36

AT NINE A.M. the meeting started in the main conference room at Texmar. Tall windows spilled the downtown Houston skyline around the room. A fifty-foot oak table was in the center of the room and thirty plush leather chairs with tall backs surrounded it.

Amanda and Tiffany sat together with Cole and Katherine sitting next to them.

Matt and Marty sat on the other side of the table across from the others.

Three attorneys had their briefcases open and occupied one end of the conference table. The senior partner of the law firm opened the meeting. "Ladies and gentleman my name is Preston Van Horn. We are here for the reading of Martin Wentworth's trust. His wishes are specific and spelled out very clear. With that being said I will now read the Wentworth trust."

The attorney took a drink of water before he began.

Several minutes went by with the attorney reading legal wording that no one understood except the attorneys. But finally the trust got specific.

"To my beautiful wife, Amanda, I leave the Southern Star Ranch and all of my personal belongings. She owns ten percent of Texmar company stock now and I leave her ten percent more of Texmar company stock."

Amanda cried and Tiffany comforted her.

The attorney waited a moment. "To my oldest son, Justin. I leave one dollar."

Matt and Marty whispered to each other.

"To my oldest daughter, Katherine. She received ten percent of Texmar company stock on her twenty-first birthday. I leave her an additional ten percent of Texmar stock."

Katherine did not react.

The attorney cleared his throat and read on. “To my son, Marty. Marty owns ten percent of Texmar stock and I leave him fifteen percent more.”

Marty and Matt shook hands and smiled at each other.

“To my youngest daughter, Tiffany. I leave her ten percent of Texmar company stock.” Tiffany cried and it was Amanda’s turn to comfort her.

Katherine squeezed her hand.

“To my brother, Matthew. In addition to the ten percent of Texmar stock that he owns, I leave fifteen percent more and appoint him temporary President and CEO until the board can elect a president or CEO to run the company.”

Matt and Marty shook hands.

The attorney continued. “The remaining ten percent of the stock will be presented to the next president of the company at the completion of a two year consecutive period. Ladies and gentleman that concludes this reading. You will all have some papers to sign. I speak for my colleagues in saying that we offer our condolences to the entire Wentworth family. We will all miss Martin enormously here at Texmar. Thank you all very much.” The attorneys placed paperwork in front of each family member.

When Matt signed the papers, he came over to Cole. “Cole, do you think we could speak in private a minute?”

“I don’t know why not.”

Matt motioned to his office and the two of them left the room with Katherine glued to their every move.

"Care for a drink?" Matt made a move toward the bar.

"I'll have a whiskey."

Matt made the drinks; they both sat down, and touched glasses.

Cole checked out the luxurious office. "I guess you must be happy about the stock that Martin left you."

"I'm anything but happy right now." Matt shot down his whiskey and poured him another.

"Really? If I had just inherited three hundred million dollars I would be celebrating."

Matt walked back and looked Cole straight in the eye. "The truth is, I'm scared to death of what might happen. Martin set the company up for disaster before he died. Even though I didn't agree with everything he was doing, I'll still be implicated for it."

"I think we should get Katherine involved in this before you say too much, Matt. She knows more about the company than I do."

"Okay, whatever. I'm just not prepared to take the heat for something that I never wanted to happen."

Cole had Katherine in the room in a matter of minutes and she could tell that her uncle was nervous.

Matt looked up at her when she came in. "Katherine, I want you to know that I was against everything I'm about to tell you."

Katherine threw a glance at Cole. "Matt, anyone knows that my father controlled this company and everything it did."

Cole made Katherine a whiskey and handed it to her.

Matt stood up. "God, how did it ever come to this?" Matt drank more whiskey. "I could go to prison. That scares me to death."

Katherine came over and held Matt's hand. "Tell us what happened, Uncle Matt."

Matt paused a moment. "Your father was good at making money in the trucking business. We turned Texmar into a giant in the industry. But it was never enough for him and soon he turned to let's say more creative ways of bringing in more cash. I'm talking billions of dollars and all cash if you can believe it. It wasn't long before it dominated all of our time and we found ourselves in the smuggling business instead of the legitimate trucking business. I never thought it would go this far, but soon it was the biggest part of our revenue."

"So what was Martin smuggling, Matt?" Cole asked.

Matt looked like a broken man. "Stolen art, treasures from third world countries wanting money for weapons. We moved everything from crowns that the early Russian czar's had worn to priceless Faberge eggs, you name it."

"So he smuggled art and treasure but who did he sell it to?" Katherine was curious.

Matt looked at her like she should know. "The highest bidder of course."

"Are you serious, Matt?" Cole asked.

"Do you know what kind of profit he was making? People want these things for their private collections and will pay almost anything to get what they couldn't normally buy on the open market."

Katherine looked at her uncle. "Do you mean to tell me he was smuggling artifacts in and delivering them around the United States?"

"He delivered them anywhere they needed to go with Texmar trucks."

"I knew he was smuggling something but I never thought that it would be anything like that." Katherine sat down in an overstuffed chair. "What did he use my island for?"

"It was a drop off point for the cargo. We picked it up with our boats afterward then took it to the docks and loaded it on our trucks for delivery. We referred to it as special cargo."

"I would have never guessed that's what he was doing there." Katherine said.

Matt was nervous. "Now that Martin is gone, it's my ass they'll come after for all of it. I don't have the political connections like he had. I don't mind telling you I'm scared to death of going to jail."

Cole stood up. "I think you should go to the FBI, Matt. I know an agent who can help us and I can call him right now."

Katherine spoke up. "I agree. You have to let them know right away or the company will go down with you. He used Texmar trucks for delivery and that involves the company."

"I'll tell them everything but they have to keep me out of jail." Matt rubbed his hands together.

"That's not up to me, Matt, but you'll have a better chance if you cooperate with them and come clean now," Cole said.

Matt looked at him. "There's something else, Cole. I'm the temporary president of Texmar until the stockholders vote for a new president in two weeks. I'm casting my vote for you."

When Cole looked at Katherine, she was smiling at him. "What! I thought that you and Marty would run Texmar."

"The boy needs a road map to find his ass. He can't run a business like this. You know the trucking business and I don't want the headaches. We can run a good trucking company, if Katherine could get along without you that is."

Katherine looked at Cole. "Matt's got twenty five percent of the stock and I have twenty. Mom and Tiffany have another thirty between them and will vote with our recommendation. I think your choice for a new president of Texmar is perfect, Uncle Matt."

"What about the hotel? I thought you wanted to run Texmar. Katherine, do you know what you're saying?"

"I'll miss you on the island but you're needed here now, Cole. You and Matt will make a great team and can make Texmar a great company. Besides, I have other plans after I finish the hotel," Katherine said.

Cole looked surprised. "I have to tell you I didn't expect this but I would love to have the job. First thing we have to do is get with the FBI and clear up the illegal business and get it out of the company. We'll fight hard for immunity for you, Matt. How's our legal staff here?"

"We have the top attorneys in the state." Matt smiled at Katherine.

"They'll earn their money for the next year or so. Let's turn this over to them right now and get the ball rolling on this thing." Cole looked a little shocked.

Katherine brought the whiskey bottle over and filled their glasses. "Gentlemen, I can already tell this is going to work. To the success of the great company that Texmar is about to become."

37

KATHERINE PULLED HER Jaguar XJL into the driveway of Benito Viatsi's home and reviewed the surroundings that she had seen two weeks ago.

The Mexican butler opened the door and Katherine handed her gun to him. The butler smiled at her, took her pistol, and led her to the library.

Benito stood up as she entered the room. "Ah, Miss Wentworth. You brighten my home with your presence."

"Hello, Benito."

"Please sit down. May I offer you a drink?"

"Whiskey on the rocks, please."

The servant handed her and Benito each a drink and closed the doors behind him.

He looked at her and smiled. "I'm glad you came. We need to get our facts straight."

"Oh yah, we need to talk, Benito. I want to know if you planted that bomb on my father's jet."

"Katherine, you came to me only a few weeks ago and told me that you had nothing to do with your father and our business was separate from his." He used several hand gestures.

"I want to know what kind of person I'm dealing with."

"You knew what kind of person I was before you dealt with me, don't tell me any different. You had better get used to it because you are in my world now!" It was the first time he had raised his voice to her. "I suppose you will tell me that you want out of our hotel deal now that your father is out of the picture?"

"I didn't come here to get out of the deal, Benito. I came here because I want some insurance."

He laughed. "Insurance? Why would you need that?"

"It seems that people are dying all around me and I don't want to get started on this project again and have someone pop you. That would leave me holding the bag on an unfinished hotel." She drank her whiskey.

"You don't have to worry about that. I have more protection than the President of the United States does. No one could possibly get to me."

"Oh Really? You have a lot of enemies and I find it hard to believe that you can protect yourself twenty-four hours a day. Do you see the situation I would be in if you were dead? I don't want to back out of this deal, but I want some insurance in case you wind up like my father."

"I assure you that my security is the very best and I put my life in their hands every day. This should be the least of your worries."

"If you're so sure then let me have the option of buying the hotel back from your family in case something does happen. That way I can still carry on with the project and not have my island tied up with a half built hotel."

He smiled. "You don't plan on putting out a hit on me, do you, Katherine?"

Katherine laughed. "How stupid do you think I am, Benito?" She drank her drink.

"This situation with your father could cloud your judgment."

"If you're so confident in your security then give me the option in our contract." She was silent.

"You really are worried about this aren't you?"

She maintained eye contact with him. "Damn straight I am. I've had my share of trouble with this hotel and I don't want any more."

"I can see where you might be concerned and I will honor your request. However, if someone does pop me, as you say, I will give you the hotel free and clear. That's how confident I am of my security." He drank and smiled again.

"That's crazy. I only asked for the option so I won't be stuck with a dead investor. You don't have to prove anything; I'll pay back the two hundred million. I just want to make sure I deal directly with you, that's all."

"Believe me; you'll never collect on the deal. But if it makes you more confident about our arrangement then it is a fair request. I will instruct my attorneys to put it in our agreement."

"Then we have a hotel to build and I can sleep again."

Benito raised his glass to hers. "To.... I just realized we don't have a name yet."

"I was going to call it the Yellow Rose." She looked to see his reaction.

To the Yellow Rose Hotel."

Their glasses touched and they both drank to it.

"You know, Katherine, I wasn't even sure, until you came over today, that we still had a deal. I hadn't heard from you since you left a couple of weeks ago."

"My father died, Benito. My family has been grieving and we need to comfort each other right now. Besides, I still think you planted that bomb. How did you expect me to react?"

"I can't discuss this business about your father but I must say I'm glad that we will build this hotel project together. I take business seriously and I wouldn't want any hard feelings between you and I over this."

"As bad as my father treated me, I wouldn't have wished him dead. That might be the way your world works, Benito, but not mine. We're business partners only and I don't wish to bring up the subject of my father again. That's all you and I will ever be." She stood up.

"I had hoped we could have more than that, Katherine. I have grown very fond of you and want to be more than just business partners." He stood up and moved closer to her.

"We're business partners and let's leave it at that. Like you said, Benito, I knew who you were before I came here." She walked to the double doors.

"I won't quit asking, you know. I happen to think you are worth chasing after." He stood there like a fine Italian gentleman that he appeared to be on the surface.

Katherine opened one of the tall doors and turned towards Benito, “Don’t chase after something you can’t catch.”

38

AT FIVE P.M. Cole rang the doorbell of the main house at the Southern Star Ranch.

The butler opened the door. “Good afternoon, Mr. Tyler. Please come in, it’s good to see you again, sir.”

“Hi, William. Hey, I heard a good one yesterday. Do you know how they make holy water?” Cole paused a second. “They boil the hell out of it.”

They both laughed.

Amanda Wentworth entered the room and smiled at Cole. "Thank you for coming on such short notice, Cole. I know you're busy and I appreciate your time."

"Mrs. Wentworth, I always have time for you." Cole liked Amanda.

"Would you walk with me, Cole?"

"It would be a pleasure, ma'am."

They walked to her greenhouse that was just outside the side door of the main house.

Amanda was still a beautiful woman for her age. "I come here to escape. The flowers are so beautiful and seem to cleanse the soul."

"This is spectacular, Mrs. Wentworth." Cole was amazed at how well she grew everything. He closed his eyes and smelled a rose. "You're right. It does cleanse the soul."

She changed to a more serious tone. "Katherine and Matt tell me that you should be the one to run Texmar. They have nothing but good things to say about you."

"Matt hit me with this bombshell at the reading of Martin's trust last week. I've got to tell you, I'm still in shock about it."

"Well, I won't tell you that I know a lot about business, Cole, because I don't. What I do know, for the first time since Texmar was founded, someone other than a Wentworth will be at the helm." She opened a drawer and pulled out a bottle of Tennessee whiskey and two glasses. "I keep this around in case the flowers don't do the trick."

He smiled at her and poured the whiskey in the glasses. They touched glasses and drank together.

"Do you object to me running the company?" Cole looked for her reaction.

"I know that Martin wanted Marty to run the company. Matt and Katherine assured me that he isn't capable of it. I don't object to you running the company, Cole. What I want you to realize though, the future of Martin's company is in your hands." She wiped a tear coming to her eye.

Cole held her hand and looked her in the eyes. "Don't think for one minute I haven't thought about that and a hundred other things. This is the toughest job I've ever had in my life. It scares me to death to even think about the shoes that I have to fill. But with the help of the Wentworth family, we can make Texmar a great company. We can even surpass Martin's dream of what he expected the company would become. I can do the job, Mrs. Wentworth, but I need the whole family behind me to do it."

"I knew in my heart that you would say that. At least I had hoped so. I know that Martin had some shady things going on. Matt told me that you have been working with the FBI and not to worry about it. Tell me, Cole, is it serious enough to destroy the company?"

"Yes, it's serious enough. We're in a battle for two things right now. Number one is survival of the company and the other is to keep Matt out of jail." Cole finished his drink.

"You're a good man, Cole. I also believe that you are a good choice as president of Texmar. Now can I ask you something that's none of my damn business?" She smiled at him when she said it.

"How could I say no to you?"

"I can see the way you and Katherine look at each other. What I can't figure out is why the two of you haven't gotten together yet."

"It's complicated, Mrs. Wentworth." He looked at the ground not knowing what to say to her.

"I'd like for you to call me Amanda because we're going to be seeing a lot of each other from now on. Okay?"

"Yes, I'd like that, Amanda."

"Let me bore you with one story before you leave. When I first dated Martin we once had a big fight about something stupid, like fights usually are. We didn't talk for a week. I didn't know if he would ever call me again so I called him. In those days it was unheard of for a girl to call a boy, but I did it anyway. We talked it through and eventually ended up getting married. I asked him once if he would have ever called and made up with me. He said he had too much pride. My point is, Cole, if I hadn't called Martin and talked to him, we wouldn't have had all of those wonderful years together. Communicating with each other is so important. Sometimes you only have one shot at real love in your life. If there are problems between you and Katherine, talk with her about it. You might have some pretty wonderful years ahead of you."

"Amanda, I would like nothing more than to be with Katherine. But Martin told me something a few months ago that confused me. I guess there's no easy way to tell you but come right out and say it. He told me that he was my real father. He and my mother had an affair and I was the result of it."

Amanda looked confused. "Oh my." She poured more whiskey for them. "That is complicated."

"I haven't told Katherine yet because I'm trying to find out if it's true. It's pure hell for me to even be around Katherine knowing I could be her half brother. I'm sorry if that upset you."

"I'm the one who asked you about it. That's what I get for nosing into your business. I always knew Martin was fooling around but I never wanted to admit it. Still, he was good to me. I hope you'll talk with Katherine and let her know what's going on."

"You're right, Amanda. It's not fair to her. I'll talk to her about it."

"Thanks, Cole. I can't bare to see any of my children suffer."

They walked back in the house and Katherine and William were in the kitchen.

"Hey there, cowboy. So you're the one who kidnapped my mother."

Cole smiled at Katherine. "I wanted to see her famous roses."

"I'll leave you two alone. He's heard me babble enough for one day. Thanks for the walk, Cole." Amanda kissed him on the cheek.

"Why do I feel like it was more than you seeing my mother's roses?" Katherine asked.

"We talked about a few things. You've got a great mom, you know. I really like her."

"Yah, I kind of like her too. Now will you tell me what you talked about or am I going to have to torture you to find out."

"I'll take the torture. It sounds like it could be fun." He pulled her close and kissed her on the lips for the first time in two months. It felt right to him but the thought was still in the back of his mind. "We have to talk about something."

"Okay, you look so serious, Cole."

He looked into her gorgeous blue eyes, "It's as serious as it gets."

39

WHEN THE DOOR to the main house opened the gunshot sent Katherine and Cole diving face down on the front porch.

Cole looked the situation over and shouted to Katherine. "We have to get over to the other side of the porch to get cover! Crawl Katherine! We have to crawl over there!" He pointed to where they needed to go.

Katherine crawled with him and another bullet whizzed over their heads.

"I'll kill you, you son of a bitch!" The man's voice said, while another bullet landed above their heads.

"What do you want?" Cole yelled. He held Katherine close and tried to shelter her.

"I want you dead is what I want." The voice said.

Inside the house, Amanda instructed William to call the police.

"Its Marty and he sounds pretty drunk." Cole told Katherine.

"Oh no. I was afraid Marty might do something stupid but not like this."

"Let's see who rules now hotshot! Show yourself or are you a coward? Some president you are. You're nothing but a coward!" Marty slurred his words. He was shouting as loud as he could and spilled whiskey on himself from the bottle as he drank. He shot wildly again at the front of the house.

"You know your sister could get hit the way you're firing. A bullet could go through the house and even hit your mother, Marty!" Cole yelled back at him.

"Screw um'! They don't care about me. You can all go to hell for all I care. You're not even a Wentworth but they want you to run the damn company. Screw all of you!" He fired again.

Cole looked at Katherine. “God, how long does it take for the cops to get here?”

A ranch hand slowly worked around one side of Marty with a long stick.

“You’re going to jail Marty unless you put that gun down!” Cole yelled and the wood splintered just above their heads and showered them with debris. “That’s six shots and I think that’s all he’s got.” He told Katherine.

“Don’t tell me you’re going out there and leaving me here.” She looked at him with uncertainty in her eyes.

“I’m not that brave, darlin’.”

The ranch hand swung the long stick and hit Marty in the head. The gun came out of his hand and he yelled with pain. He kicked the gun away and swung the stick again across Marty’s face. Marty went down and didn’t get up.

The police arrived with red lights flashing and sirens blaring and took Marty into custody.

Cole got up from the porch but Katherine stayed down.

She looked surprised. “I just bought this outfit and now look at it.”

Cole looked down and saw a spot of blood on her chest.

“Oh my God! Katherine, are you hit?”

“Yah, I guess I am. I better go see the doc’.”

“Lay down right here, sweetheart. Hey! Call an ambulance! She’s been shot! Hurry!”

The police officer came running up on the porch to help. "We've got an ambulance coming. How bad is it?"

"It's near her heart." Cole held her in his arms.

She looked at him with dazed eyes. "I like it when you call me sweetheart.

"Okay sweetheart, the ambulance will take you to the hospital and everything will be fine. I won't leave you, Katherine. Where's that damn ambulance?" He yelled at the police officer.

Amanda cried and William held her away.

The ambulance rushed in and the attendants came with a gurney. They took her vital signs and had the hospital on the radio.

Cole stepped back and hugged Amanda.

The attendants put Katherine on the gurney and loaded her inside the ambulance.

"William, bring Amanda to the hospital. Okay? I'm going in the ambulance." Cole yelled.

The doors of the ambulance closed and sped away.

Cole looked in Katherine's blue eyes and held her hand as the paramedics tried to stabilize her. He closed his eyes and somehow wished he could wake up from this nightmare. But when he opened them, Katherine was still in the ambulance fighting for her life.

40

THE HOSPITAL WAITING room was filled with people worrying about Katherine.

Amanda and Tiffany held hands and prayed that she would be all right.

Cole paced back and forth impatiently.

Wendy Taggert and her husband talked with the ranch hand that swatted the gun out of Marty's hand.

The table in the waiting room was littered with empty paper coffee cups that they consumed from the long wait. It seemed they had been there an eternity when the door opened and the doctor appeared.

"Hello everyone, I'm Doctor Keller. Katherine's condition is good considering what she has gone through.

"The bullet missed her heart by one inch, and fortunately, didn't damage any vital organs. We stopped some internal bleeding and the x-rays indicate that no bullet fragments remain. She will be in recovery for two to three hours and will be moved into her room afterwards. Katherine is a very lucky woman and I expect a full recovery. Any questions I can answer for you?" The doctor smiled.

The room came alive with hugs and smiles.

Cole hugged Amanda and Tiffany. "We're so lucky to still have her."

"I couldn't imagine life without her." Amanda wiped the tears from her face."

"We're lucky to have you too, Cole." Tiffany kissed him on the cheek.

"Thanks, Tiffany. That means a lot to me to have you say that." Cole smiled at her. "She's going to be in recovery for three hours. How about I buy you gals some dinner and we'll come back afterwards?"

"You know, Tiffany, I think Cole has already begun to talk like a Texan. What do you think?" Amanda asked.

"I think if I a little older I'd chase after you myself."

They all laughed and headed out of the hospital.

After two hours in the recovery room, Katherine began to awaken, but she saw blurry and distorted images. A man in a white coat held her chart. Although the image was still not clear, she swore she saw the man wearing cowboy boots. When she looked at his face, she recognized her older brother and spoke to him in a whisper.

"Hey, cowboy. What brings you into town?"

It surprised, Justin, and he made eye contact with his sister. "Hey there, sis'. Long time no see." He came closer to the bed and held her hand.

"Is this a dream or are you really here?"

"I'm really here. You had a lot of people worried about you. Marty really blew it this time."

"Well, he's a lot like daddy was. He's got a temper and sometimes it gets the best of him."

"The bullet missed your heart by only an inch. You're gonna' walk out of here in a few days just fine."

"Where have you been for the last five years?"

"Away from the dictator we called father. I heard he dished you up some crap too."

"Yah. I left Texmar because I knew he wouldn't change. Did you hear about my hotel?" She was more awake.

"Sure did. I'd like to help you with it too."

She smiled at him. "Do you mean it, Justin?"

"Absolutely. Just as soon as you get out of here. I met your guy, Cole."

"Isn't he wonderful? I've had a good feeling about him ever since we met. I love him, Justin, and he doesn't even know it yet."

Justin looked at the floor and didn't say anything.

"What's wrong?" She still could read him like a book.

"What makes you think something is wrong?"

"Don't play games with me." She stared at him.

"You know, I never could keep anything from you. Even when we were younger, you could always tell when I lied. I don't think this is the time or place to tell you. Why don't you heal up a little before we go into this."

"There's no chance you're gonna' walk out that door without telling me. Now let's have it." She sat up.

"Well, at least I know if you talk like that you're not too bad off." Justin blew out a breath. "Before dad died he told Cole that he was his real father."

"What? So, that's why he's been acting so strange. But is it true or was it something that daddy made up?"

"Cole is extremely upset about it and had me look into every record I could find. I couldn't find any evidence of it anywhere. The only way to know for sure is to test Cole's DNA against dad's and that's impossible now."

"So we'll never know for sure?"

"Once he was cremated everything was gone."

"God, Justin. How did our lives become so complicated?"

"The great Martin Wentworth has still managed a way to dominate ours lives even in death."

"I believe that people come into your life for a reason. Cole and I belong together. I have to find out because the rest of my life depends on it."

"Don't worry about it, sis'. I'll find a way. Now get some rest and I'll come back with the family to see you."

"Promise?" She didn't want to let go of his hand.

"Yes. Now close those eyes and get better. We have a hotel to build."

"Thanks, Justin."

"For what? I haven't done anything yet."

"For coming back home. Our family isn't complete without you."

Justin blew her a kiss and shut the door. He came face to face with Cole. It startled him for a moment. "God, Cole! You scared the shit out of me."

"Good, it's about time I paid you back. Are you playing doctor or is white lab coat a new fashion?

"I was worried about her. By the way, what are you doing here?"

"Actually, I was looking for a way in too. She means everything to me, Justin." Cole opened the door and found Katherine asleep. He smiled and shut the door satisfied that she was okay.

"Cole, lets go someplace and talk."

"Yah, I need something take my mind off of this."

They made their way to the cafeteria and found a table where no one could hear them.

"Okay, what did you find out, Justin?"

"As far as Martin being your father, I found no record anywhere that proves it. Your birth records show exactly what your mother told you. Your father died when you were four years old."

"I wish this could be proven one way or the other. It's the uncertainty that haunts me." Cole looked around the room.

"There's something else I thought about. My father mentioned all of his children in his will but not you. Don't you think that's a little strange?"

"Strange yes, but it still doesn't prove anything. Keep digging, Justin. We've got to solve this thing so that Katherine and I can get on with our lives."

Justin looked around the room again, "I found out something else about the company that you should know about, Cole."

"I'm listening."

"About six or seven months ago Texmar had some trucks hijacked. I found out it was the Viatsi family. When Viatsi found out what my father was smuggling, he wanted in on the action."

"Martin hated him. Why would he let him in on the action? He didn't need him."

Justin looked around again. "Yeah but once Viatsi knew the amount of money involved, he had to have a piece. My father probably thought that he could pop Viatsi once his guard was down."

"But you think Viatsi killed him first so that he could take over the operation?"

"Think about it. He controls the island now too."

Cole looked disgusted, "I'm afraid Viatsi is going to be more trouble than we can handle."

Justin shrugged his shoulders. "It wouldn't hurt to have your FBI friend check it out. By the way, how will Matt come out of all of this?"

"We still hope to keep him out of jail but he had to squeal on a lot of people. I worry about how long we can keep him alive once he tells it all."

"Uncle Matt will never live his life in the witness protection program. I know him well enough to know that."

"Yeah I know, Justin. I also know that jail scares him to death. Your father left him in a bad situation."

"I wanted to tell you that I told Katherine today I would help her with the hotel. It worries me that Viatsi is her partner. I'm afraid he thinks she'll be an easy target once he doesn't need her."

"Good, she needs all the help she can get now that I'll be running Texmar.

"You really care about her?"

"I feel like we belong together."

"Funny, she said the same thing today when I was in her room. You really do belong with her, Cole."

"I was afraid that I might have lost her today, Justin. I haven't told her that I love her because I wasn't sure under the circumstances if I should. But I thought she might die and never know. So when I see her I'm going to tell her."

"I've got my work cut out for me. Two lives depend on what I come up with. I'll talk with you soon." Justin left the cafeteria.

Cole made his way back up to Katherine's private room. When he opened the door, she sat up in bed and smiled at him. He had a dozen red roses in a tall vase and sat them on the table next to her bed. "I thought I had lost you today and it really scared me." He held her hand. "I love you, Katherine and I was afraid you would never know."

"Oh, Cole." She hugged him and cried on his shoulder. "I love you too."

"It was killing me to hold it in."

"I know what daddy told you and I understand now."

"How did you find out?"

"Justin told me."

"Did he tell you that he's helped me all along?"

"No, but he's always been there for me and I thought he might somehow be watching out for me. Cole, promise me something. Promise me that no matter how this family thing turns out, you'll always be a part of my life."

Cole looked into her deep blue eyes, "I promise."

41

SEVEN MONTHS HAD passed since Cole and Katherine knew how they felt about each other. She recovered quickly and was on the job site everyday to see that her hotel became a reality. It stood on the very spot that she and Cole had drawn in the sand over a year ago.

Her cell phone rang. “Hello, Katherine Wentworth.”

“Good morning, Katherine.”

“What do you want, Benito?” Katherine frowned.

"Not even a good morning from you? Is there something bothering you?"

"Yah, you bother me. What do you want?"

"Such an unpleasant way to greet me."

"Cut to the chase, Benito, I'm busy."

"Well if you insist on being rude then I guess I'll have to get right down to business. I want to visit the hotel to see the progress."

"I told you it wouldn't be ready for you to look at until next month."

"Unacceptable. I will arrive at eight this evening and will expect you to be there."

"Look, I don't take orders from you. If you come to see this hotel tonight then you can show yourself around."

"You need to show me some respect. I have killed people for less than that!" He raised his voice.

"Benito, you're on a cell phone and anyone could be listening. I'll say it again so you can clearly understand this time. If you come tonight, you're on your own. If your English is not good enough to understand that then get one of your goons to translate it for you!" Katherine broke the connection and threw her cell phone in the sand.

Justin walked up from behind her and picked up her phone. "Bad news?"

"Thanks, Justin." She took the phone from him. "It's

always bad news when Viatsi calls."

"What's that little weasel want now?"

"He's wants to see the hotel but I'm not ready for him yet. He doesn't like to be told what to do. He reminds me of daddy in some ways. He doesn't care about anyone but himself and wants to control everything." She watched the surf crash into the shore a hundred yards away.

"I can't believe we have to let that slime ball take over this place."

"Tell me about it."

Justin sighed. "What can we do to get it back? Can we buy him out?"

"I wish it were that easy. Viatsi knew he had me in an awkward position when I went to him. It was an easy move for him and he is not about to let it go now."

Justin paused then looked at her. "Something isn't right with this deal. If you were dad, wouldn't you know that Viatsi would be the only possibility you had left? He had closed off all of the other sources of capital for you, right?"

"Yeah, but they hated each other."

"Still, he had to know that you would go to him because that was your last resort. Don't you think that he and Viatsi could have planned the buyout together?"

"I don't think they could get along well enough to do business. That's the reason I went to Viatsi for help."

"They might have hated each other but they have done business together before."

"What!" Katherine was surprised.

"The Viatsi family hijacked four trucks from Texmar a while back."

"Yes, I remember it, but I didn't know they had anything to do with it."

"I dug up a few things that might surprise you."

"So what kind of business did they do together?" She was curious.

"Viatsi found out what they were smuggling and dad cut him in on the action to keep him quiet."

Katherine looked shocked. "Surely you're kidding?"

"They did hate each other but dad would do almost anything for the right business deal. If he made a deal with Viatsi, the old man could end up being your partner without you even knowing."

She thought for a minute then put her hand on her head. "How could I be so stupid? What's even scarier, he almost got away with it."

"Almost or did he get away with it?"

"What do you mean?" Katherine looked at him.

"Dad could get away with things that most people couldn't dream of. I found hundreds of millions he stashed away in off shore accounts. I believe he might not be dead after all."

"Justin, you can't be serious." You don't think he could stoop that low do you?"

"It's the old man, sis'. What would make you think he couldn't?"

Katherine thought about it. "But the medical examiner positively identified the remains."

"That's the reason I believe he might have staged his own death. The medical examiner identified a tooth as positive proof of his death. I talked with all three divers that brought up the remains from the gulf. Not one of them brought up any teeth."

"God, Justin, you don't really think..."

"I'm just saying we shouldn't rule it out." Justin looked his sister straight in the eye. "There is something we could do to smoke him out if he's still alive."

"I don't know if I want to know, but tell me anyway."

"I could move the money out of the off shore accounts and hide it. I'll guarantee, if he's still out there, he'll come looking for his money."

"You know how to do that?"

"Oh, sis', I can do all kinds of things that you don't want to know about."

"Can't he trace the money and find out who took it?"

"Not the way I'll do it. I'll bounce it around the globe a few times before I make it completely disappear. But you realize he'll suspect us eventually. After all, that's the idea."

"Have any withdrawals been made on the money since his death?"

"That's what got me suspicious. Three days ago, twenty million dollars was withdrawn and the transaction was encrypted so no one could trace it. No one except me, of course."

"And where did it end up?" Katherine asked.

"Ready for this? Right here in Houston, Texas."

"Oh My God. Everything you just told me could have happened. Cole and I would finally know the truth if he was alive."

"Don't get your hopes up. It's a long shot at best."

"Hey, I bet on long shots remember?"

"If he's still out there somewhere, let's bring him to us and solve this mystery once and for all."

"Are you sure you won't get caught?"

"It's not my style to get caught."

"Why do my senses tell me this is a bad idea?"

"Would you rather him show up as the owner of your hotel when you finish it? How would that make you feel?"

Katherine looked at the water and then back at her brother. "This is so scary, Justin, but I don't see that we have any other choice."

42

TWELVE HUNDRED TEXMAR employees gathered on the eleventh floor of the Wentworth building.

Matt walked on the stage and introduced Cole as the new president of Texmar.

Cole received a loud applause as he made his way to the microphone and shook Matt's hand. He gave Katherine and Amanda a wink before he spoke. "Thank you all for that warm welcome. I know that most of you probably don't know who I am. Well, I'll tell you right off that I'm not

Martin Wentworth and I won't even try to be. What I will tell you, next year at this time, you will not only know me better, but you'll like to work for Texmar a lot more than you do right now."

The crowd whispered to each other.

"Teamwork and happy employees make a successful company." Cole looked his audience over carefully.

"I once had a secretary that gave me her notice and I couldn't for the life of me figure out why. So, I asked her why because I really liked her work. She said that a third of her wages went for day care for her two children. After she paid for gas and lunches, she only had a few hundred dollars a week left. Then she asked me if I would work all week for a few hundred bucks. Sometimes a boss gets so far removed from the employee that they don't think about these things. After asking more employees about it, I found that several people were in the same boat. So, I got the best people I could find and I started a daycare facility right on the premises. My secretary stayed and I noticed that people actually started smiling at me.

"Starting today, I will turn the nineteenth floor of this building to into a daycare facility staffed with top qualified people. This service will be free of charge as long as you are an employee of this company."

The employees applauded and whistled.

Cole waited for the applause to subside.

"If you liked that then you're really gonna' like this. As of today we will start a profit sharing plan so that every employee is rewarded for the profits that the whole company makes."

That comment got even more applause by the crowd. Whistles filled the large auditorium and conveyed the employee's approval.

Cole continued. "See what I mean, you're happier all ready. Ladies and gentlemen, welcome to the new Texmar."

The applause and whistles were so loud; it took a full minute to die down.

Cole smiled at Katherine and looked back at the crowd. "I started out as a truck driver in this business more than twenty years ago. I know what it's like to have someone promise you that you're going home and then say you have another run when you get done. This will not happen with me at the helm. We'll have enough drivers so our people don't fall asleep at the wheel and don't have to cheat on their logbooks.

"Some of my executives will say that's not possible. Believe me, we'll make it happen. I guarantee that our drivers will be a lot happier and stay with the company a lot longer."

More applause came from the crowd.

"I've been in the trucking business a long time but I still don't have all of the answers. I need your help to make Texmar so successful that the competition won't be able to touch us. I want to make Texmar such a great company that you won't want to work for anyone else.

"Your new ideas are welcome and encouraged. I don't care if you're sweeping floors and come up with a better way to route freight; I want to hear about it. By the way, more money flows to you if you come up with an idea that works for us. Why not, it saves the company money."

Again, the employees applauded.

"My philosophy for this company is not complicated. If we work together as a real team, we can dominate the trucking industry. I have no doubt that our competition will wonder how we do it. All I ask of you is do your job the very best you can and make our company run as efficient as possible. If we have twelve thousand people that think as one, how can we lose? I'm honored to be your new president of Texmar."

Every person in the large room stood up and cheered for Cole's speech.

Katherine gave Cole a big hug as he stepped away from the microphone.

Cole hugged Amanda and he saw tears in her eyes. He shook some of the top executive's hands. He raised both of his hands with Katherine and Matt's, and the audience applauded even more. It was the response he had hoped for.

After a few minutes, he came off stage and Amanda, Katherine, and Matt followed him. They made their way through the crowd and got into the private elevator.

"Wow! I was hoping for that kind of response," Cole said.

Amanda smiled at him. "You made a lot of people very happy."

"I don't think daddy ever got that kind of applause," Katherine said.

"Now comes the hard part. You have to deliver on your promises," Matt said.

"Well' no one said it would be easy. I have to have all of the employees on my side to accomplish these things. I believe in what I said today and I'm putting my reputation at stake right off the bat."

The elevator doors opened and all of them walked into his new office.

To everyone's surprise, Justin was waiting for them.

Amanda hugged him. "Oh Justin, I still can't believe that you're back."

"I hate to spoil your celebration but I have some bad news."

"Does everyone need to hear this, Justin?" Katherine asked.

"Why not, it'll be on the news in a few hours anyway. Benito Viatsi was killed last night." Justin looked at Katherine.

She looked shocked. "What? You can't be serious."

"How was he killed?" Cole asked.

"Someone hung him. Anyone care for a drink?" Justin walked toward the bar.

"Whiskey." Matt loosened his tie.

"Where, Justin?" Katherine asked.

"On the island, sis'. Someone hung him off the fourth floor of the hotel." Justin poured whiskey into a few glasses then looked up at her.

"God no! They'll think I had something to do with it." Katherine put her hand over her mouth in disbelief.

Amanda turned to her daughter. "But you were at the ranch last night with Cole and me, honey."

"It won't matter, mama. I made a contract with Viatsi because I thought something like this might happen." Katherine looked worried.

Cole blew out a breath. "What kind of contract?"

"I wanted to guarantee that I had enough money to build the hotel. So, I made an agreement with Viatsi that if someone killed him I would still get my money to build it. I didn't want to be left with a dead investor. I was afraid that daddy might have him killed because he financed my hotel."

"So, you made a good business decision. How does that make you a suspect?" Matt sipped his whiskey.

"Viatsi was so sure of his security that he said I could have the two hundred million if someone killed him. I didn't know that someone actually would."

"That does make you look bad. It gives you motive, a lot of motive," Matt said.

Katherine looked out the window at downtown Houston. "I knew he was trouble. I should have known not to get involved in a business deal with him."

Amanda walked up to her. "You have a solid alibi, honey."

"Don't you see, mama? They'll still think I had someone do it."

Justin took a drink of his whiskey. "What do you think, Cole?"

"I think it's a little too convenient that Katherine had this deal with Viatsi and then he gets murdered on the island. It's a set up and I don't want to even think about who could be behind it." Cole looked at Katherine and then Justin. "Do you know any more details about it, Justin?"

"Well, I didn't want to gross you out or anything. But it's obvious he was tortured before he died."

"I'm sorry I don't take these kinds of things well. If you all don't mind I'll go back to the ranch." Amanda put her hand on Katherine's. "Please don't worry about this, honey. I'm sure it will come out fine."

"Thanks, mama. Will you be all right?" Katherine asked.

"Of course I will," Amanda said.

"I'll call Tommy for you, Amanda, and I'll walk you to the limo." Matt dialed the phone and escorted her out.

"Okay, Justin. How was he tortured?" Cole sipped his drink.

"All of his fingernails were pulled out and some of his fingers were cut off. Someone wanted information from him before they killed him." Justin poured another drink.

"Who would have the nerve to kill Benito Viatsi?" Katherine asked. "The guy has got an army of security people."

Cole looked at Justin and then at Katherine.

The room was silent.

"Oh my God!" Katherine broke the silence. "This has got to be a nightmare. Justin, he wanted information out of Viatsi."

Cole looked at both of them. "What are you talking about. What kind of information?"

"I bet I know." Justin looked at Katherine.

"You were right. Daddy wants his money and he would definitely kill for that," Katherine said.

Cole rolled his eyes. "What did you do with Martin's money, Justin?"

"I temporarily moved it out of his accounts."

Cole put his hand up to his forehead. "How much of it did you move?"

"I took all two hundred million. I wanted to see if he faked his own death."

Cole walked to the window and turned to face both of them. "Then I guess you have your answer. The question is, who do you think he'll come after next?"

43

FIFTEEN BLACK LIMOUSINES lined the road at the cemetery. A hundred people gathered around Benito Viatsi's gravesite. All of them appeared to be respectable businessmen dressed in expensive suits. But most carried guns under their coats.

Several men guarded the area because the Viatsi family had many enemies.

Cole and Katherine got out of their limo and walked toward the gravesite. Viatsi security confronted them immediately.

The man opened his suit jacket to show the butt of a pistol. "Sorry, but this service is private and I can't allow you to pass."

Cole and Katherine stopped when they spotted the pistol in the man's jacket.

Katherine spoke with confidence. "Benito was my business partner. I want to pay my respects."

"May I have your name please, ma'am?"

"Katherine Wentworth."

"Please wait here and I'll ask if you can attend." The man stepped away and whispered something to one of the men at the gravesite.

He and two other men walked over to Cole and Katherine. The well-dressed man spoke with a slight Italian accent. "Miss Wentworth, I am Lafonza Viatsi. I apologize for this awkward moment, but security is very tight since my uncle's death. I hope that we didn't offend you in any way."

"Not at all, I understand completely. I offer my deepest sympathy for the loss to your family. Benito and I were business partners." Katherine tried to read him. "I'm sorry, may I introduce you to Cole Tyler."

Cole shook Lafonza's hand. "Pleasure to meet you, Mr. Viatsi, and I offer my condolences to you and your family."

"Ah, the new power figure in Houston. The pleasure is mine, Mr. Tyler, and I wish you only success with Texmar." Lafonza shook Cole's hand. He turned to Katherine. "I wonder if I could have a private word with you, Miss Wentworth?"

"Of course. I'll be right back, Cole." Katherine walked away from him.

Lafonza and Katherine walked several yards away. Two security men walked thirty feet behind them.

"Miss Wentworth, I must say my uncle thought a great deal of you. I know about your business deal with him because I helped draft it. I want you to know I advised him against it because I knew there was bad blood between your family and ours."

"I never thought that Benito would get killed, Lafonza. He was so well protected and I don't know how it happened."

"Miss Wentworth, what happened in the past is not my concern and I don't blame you. My concern is what the future holds, because I am the head of the family now. I have spent too much time at this cemetery lately. I have buried three of my family members here in the last year."

"Yes, I know that. My father was responsible for their deaths. He was also a casualty of this war."

"I think there is room for both of our families to exist without any more death. This feud between our families started with two men who are both dead. I have no quarrel with you. We must end this now or we will simply wipe both of our families out."

"I agree, Lafonza, and I'm glad you think like a businessman."

Lafonza looked deep in her eyes. "Then this thing between our families is done?"

"Yes, it is over and done."

"Thank you, Miss Wentworth. I needed to clarify my position with you. You are a friend to the Viatsi family now. The loan that my father gave you is considered paid as agreed in the contract. Although, I don't think it is wise that we conduct any future business. I will only ask one more favor from you." His expression became more serious. "My family will not welcome you to my uncle's gravesite because of our differences. I ask you to respect their wishes and pay your respects when all of them are gone."

"I will respect the wishes of your family, Lafonza." She turned around and walked toward Cole.

The three men looked at Katherine as she walked away. Even in her black funeral outfit, it was hard to look away.

Her blond hair spilled over the black dress and stopped just below her middle back. Her slim but attractive figure swayed as she walked away from them.

“Come on, let’s get out of here.” She walked past Cole.

“What was that all about?” He caught up to her.

“I guess he thinks I’m stupid. He wants me to think this is all done and we can both go back to our business as if nothing happened.”

“Well, what’s wrong with that?”

Katherine sat down in the limo. “He’ll try to kill me the first chance he gets because he thinks I’m trouble.”

“You got all of that from a few minutes with him?” Cole got in and sat down.

“It doesn’t take long to read an idiot. He’s as phony as they come and I don’t trust him.”

Cole poured them both a drink.

She put her hand on his and smiled at him. “Thanks for coming with me today.”

“Lady, I’d go anywhere with you.” He kissed her and drank his whiskey.

“I know you thought it was a bad idea, but it was important that I talked to Lafonza.” She sipped her drink.

“So you knew that he wouldn’t let you attend the funeral?”

“Not the way our two families have fought.”

"You're a gutsy one you know." Cole drank his drink down.

"I don't know about you but I'm exhausted." Katherine drank more.

"Yah, me too. I'm so tired I could take a nap."

"Cole, listen to us." She rested her head on the seat.

"Yah, I'm really tired, Katherine." Cole slurred his words and closed his eyes.

"Shit! The drink is drugged, Cole!" He got blurry. "Driver, stop the car!"

But the driver looked back and raised the smoked glass partition between him and his passengers.

"Katherine, I love you." Cole struggled to get the words out of his mouth.

"I should have been smarter than this. I love you too!" She lost consciousness.

44

KATHERINE AND COLE regained consciousness in one of the newly built bungalows on the island. They both sat in chairs with their arms tied behind them.

As Katherine's eyes slowly focused, she thought she must be dreaming when she saw her father in front of her.

Martin smiled at her. "Well hello there, sweetheart. I didn't think that you and lover boy there would ever sleep that drink off."

Katherine looked around the room and then back at him. "Daddy?"

"You know, for such a powerful business woman as yourself, you sure are easy to snatch up at a moments notice. You might want to consider some security to watch your backside."

"Well, look who rose up from the dead." Cole struggled to get his hands free of the rope without success.

"Shut up, Cole. I don't have the time to deal with you right now." Martin glared at him.

"Guess you had a good reason to fake your own death huh, daddy?"

"I sure did, darlin' and although I'd like to tell you the whole story, I'm a little pressed for time right now."

Austin stood by the door.

Katherine gave him a dirty look then looked back at her father. "You didn't even get plastic surgery. I know why too. You're afraid of the pain. You're such a pussy about things like that."

Martin laughed. "God, you still have a big mouth, little girl. I think you know why you're here and like I said, I don't really have the luxury of time. You have my money and I want it back."

"I thought you wanted to start from scratch and do it all over again for the thrill?" She said to her father.

"I heard the same thing from you, Martin," Cole said.

"I told you to keep your mouth shut, Cole. This is a family matter and you're not involved." Martin frowned at him.

Cole got angry. "Oh really, Martin. How about that little talk we had when you told me you're my real father.

"That was just a little distraction I cooked up to occupy your time. It worked just like I thought it would too. It shows that I can manipulate you any time I want." He smiled at his daughter.

Katherine looked at Cole then at her father. "I don't think you know what it's like to love someone, daddy. Cole and I went through hell because of that."

"Well I'm touched, sweetheart, but it's still not the reason I'm here," Martin said.

She gave her father a dirty look. "Go to hell and take all of your money with you."

"Did your idiot brother take my money?"

"Yeah, he took it and I'm glad he did."

"Then we need to locate him. Oh, did I mention that I've wired your hotel with explosives? You don't know the rules yet, little girl. You never mess with someone who has more money, more power and is smarter than you," Martin said.

Katherine smiled. "The way I see it, I'd say you were broke. Without the money, you have no power."

Martin smiled back and came close to her. "I came here to get my damn money back and I'm not leaving without it. Your hotel is gone no matter what, but if you want Cole to live, then you had better find a way to get my money back."

Cole looked at her. "Don't even consider it, Katherine. I'd sooner die than give him a penny."

"It's not up to you so don't waste your breath. No, our ambitious girl will decide if you live or die today." Martin turned to Katherine. "What's it gonna' be, darlin'?"

"If I could save Cole's life, I would give the money back to you in a second. You see, daddy, I love him and his life is worth much more to me than any amount of money. You, on the other hand, traded your whole family for money. Your priorities are all screwed up. You should have done your homework because I don't know how to get your money back. Justin is the only one that can do that."

"Well, I guess lover boy goes up with the hotel then. Austin, haul his butt over there and lock him up." Martin looked at his daughter. "I want my money, sweetheart, and that's all it will take to save his life."

"I said I don't know how to get your money back. Don't do this to Cole." She pleaded.

Martin looked at Cole. "See there, Cole, she just traded a bunch of money for your life. That's what kind of a woman she is. No matter what she tells you, all she wants is that money."

"You better hope I never get out of this, Martin, because I'll strangle you myself if I do. She doesn't know how to get that money back any more than I do," Cole said.

Austin held him at gunpoint and walked towards the hotel.

Tears ran down Katherine's cheeks. "Why do you have to do this, daddy? Do you really hate me that much?"

"You know I don't play games when it comes to my money. I'll blow him to pieces and you know that. Get my money back and I'll let him live."

"Don't you understand that Justin is the only one who can do that?" She pleaded with him again.

Cole disappeared into the hotel with Austin.

"Then I suggest you get him here real quick." Martin untied her and walked Katherine to the hotel.

Katherine saw Cole handcuffed to the registration desk. "I can't contact Justin. He contacts me."

"You expect me to believe that crap?" Martin smiled at her. "I didn't get off yesterday's stage, you know."

Just then, they heard a single gunshot and Austin fell to the ground. He was shot in the heart and died instantly.

Martin reached for his pistol when another shot pierced his hand. The pistol fell to the ground and Martin yelled in pain. "Damn!" He put his other hand over the one-inch hole.

Katherine looked up and saw Justin with a rifle in his hand. "My God, Justin!" She ran and hugged him.

"Are you all right, sis'?"

"Yeah, but Cole's in the hotel locked up. Daddy put explosives in there, Justin." Tears streamed down her face.

"Okay, I'll get him out of there." Justin knocked his father down and drug him into the hotel. "Get in there you piece of shit."

Martin looked up at him. "Well, if it isn't the mystery man. Where's my money you little punk?"

Justin helped his father up and then hit him in the stomach as hard as he could.

It sent Martin back to the floor and he gasped for breath.

"That's because you gave Katherine a bad time when I was gone." Justin kicked his father in the face as he tried to get to his feet. "That's for doing this."

Martin's face was bloody and he backed away. "You don't know who you're dealing with. I'll kill you for that."

"Where's the key for those cuffs on Cole?" Justin asked his father.

Martin chuckled. "There is no key. Once those cuffs are on, they don't come off."

Justin looked at Cole's cuffs and found no keyhole. He looked at Katherine and then Cole. "He's right. They don't come off."

Katherine looked at her father. "You mean you would have killed Cole even if I had given you your money back?"

Martin laughed. "In a few minutes this whole place will be leveled anyway. Once Austin started the timer, it's impossible to turn off."

Justin looked at the amount of explosives and read the timer. "Oh shit!" He backed away from the charge that was tied to one of the main supports in the lobby of the hotel. "He's got enough explosives to level this place and less than two minutes left on the timer. We have to get out of here!"

"This whole place is wired like that. That's just one of ten charges." Martin chuckled. "Your hotel is history, honey."

Katherine hugged Cole. "We have to find a way to get Cole out of here, Justin. Please!"

Cole looked at Justin. "All of you get out of here, right now! There's nothing you can do for me."

Katherine cried and hung on to Cole. "No! No! I won't leave you, Cole! Not after we know we can live our lives together now."

"There's got to be something to free you from those cuffs around here." Justin looked around the hotel frantically.

"You would need a torch to get him out of those. There not meant to come off." Martin was still on the ground.

Justin checked the timer and it read one minute and forty seconds. He grabbed some duct tape and taped Martin's hands behind his back.

Cole looked at Justin. "There's no need for us all to die. Go with Katherine and Martin, take a boat, and get the hell out of here. There's no time to waste, Justin. Just do it!"

Katherine tried to hang on to Cole but Justin pulled her away. "No, please get him loose!"

"I wish it didn't have to be like this, Cole," Justin said.

"Turn Martin over to the FBI and watch over Katherine for me. Okay?" Cole looked at them at the door. "Better hurry."

"No, please, Justin!" Katherine pleaded. "I love you, Cole." Tears ran down her cheeks.

"I love you too!" He watched them disappear from the door.

Justin, Katherine, and Martin ran for the boats.

Justin shoved Martin and he fell in the boat. He started the motor for Katherine. "When you get to shore, turn him over to the FBI and explain what happened. Get out of here as quick as you can."

"What are you doing, Justin?" Katherine asked with tear soaked eyes.

Justin shoved them off. "I can't just leave him there. I have to see if I can free him. Now go!"

"You'll be a dead hero," Martin said to his son.

Justin ran back towards the hotel.

"If you don't shut up I'll feed you to the sharks," Katherine said. She gave the engine the gas and they sped away from the island.

The explosion happened less than a minute later and produced a spectacular fireball. It was so violent they felt the shock wave a half mile away in the boat.

Katherine immediately turned the boat around and sped back to the island, but only saw huge piles of smoking concrete and steel supports bent and twisted. Her dream hotel was completely demolished. Tears dripped off of her face as she walked over mound after mound of ruble but after hours of searching she found no signs of Justin or Cole.

45

SEVENTY TWO HOURS after the FBI took Martin into custody; he walked out of the back door of the federal building and drove away with two men. He immediately asked for a cell phone and began dialing.

His daughter answered his call sitting at Cole's desk at Texmar. "Katherine Wentworth."

"Well hello there, sweetheart. I wanted you to be the first to know that the FBI was nice enough to release me."

She looked out the window of the office. "That doesn't

surprise me at all. I know you have many corrupted friends in the FBI."

"Really, then why would you turn me over to them if you knew that I would be released?"

"Because it was the right thing to do. I can't be held responsible for anything that they do with you."

"Well, I have powerful friends, honey, and you have no idea the favors they will do for me. But my business with you isn't over because you still have my money. I'm coming after you with both barrels cocked and my finger on the trigger."

"What more can you do to me? You blew up my hotel and killed the two most important people in my life. What do I have left that you could possibly want?" She stared out at the lights of downtown Houston.

"I guess your mom and sister will have to pay for your little stunt now. I'll kill everyone, starting with them then you, unless I get my money back. Is that clear enough for you?"

"Oh, perfectly clear, daddy. I truly believe you would kill us all for your precious money."

"Then let's meet and settle this thing once and for all."

"If we did that then I would be harboring a fugitive."

"I'm no fugitive, darlin'. I told you the FBI let me go."

"How do you know that the men in the car with you are FBI agents? Did you ask to see their badges?"

"Let's stop the nonsense. This is child's play."

"Is it child's play to threaten your own family? Is it child's play to blow up a two hundred million dollar hotel and kill two people?"

Martin swallowed hard. "What's your point?"

"My point is, you're out of federal lock up and don't even know who's riding in the car with you. You know for a big, powerful businessman like yourself you sure are easy to snatch up on a moment's notice. You should consider some security to watch your backside. Sound familiar, daddy?" Katherine made herself a whiskey at the bar.

"How stupid do you think I am, darlin'?" He watched one of the men reach over the seat and handcuff him to a bar that was in the back of the squad car. "Just what the hell is going on here?"

"I gave you every chance in the world, daddy. I'm sorry it had to come to this but I can't have you threaten our family any longer. You would never let us live a normal life again. No one should have to put up with a monster like you and no one ever will again." Katherine took a swig of her whiskey and hung up the phone.

The car sped up and turned down a dusty road.

Martin pleaded to the man seated in front of him. "I don't know what she's paying you but I'll ten times the money if you stop and let me out!"

The two men in the front seat turned and smiled at each other. They drove a couple of minutes before they stopped.

Martin sat handcuffed to the bar and his heart pounded in his chest.

The two men got out of the car and left him alone.

Then the front door opened and a well-dressed Italian man spoke to Martin from the front seat. "Mr. Wentworth, I am Lafonza Viatsi."

"You mean to tell me my daughter is in business with a low life like you?"

"On the contrary, I met with her and told her that the business between our families was finished. However, she predicted you would be released and felt I could dispose of the problem for both of our families."

"I'll pay you millions if you spare my life. Tell me what your price is," Martin said.

"You really don't understand. This isn't about money, Mr. Wentworth. Unlike you, I don't think any amount of money is worth more than your family. The justice we seek will allow both of our families' peace." He got out of the seat and leaned back in. "See you in hell, Mr. Wentworth."

He shut the door and Martin shook. He heard the sound of a truck motor as it gained speed. He looked out the window and saw a tractor trailer in line for a head on collision with the car. He closed his eyes before the truck hit the car and annihilated it.

The car exploded like a bomb and pieces of metal and glass flew in every direction. The truck came around again for a second run and hit what was left of the car.

A piece of heavy equipment scooped up what the debris and shoved it off into a deep hole. Then it moved mounds of rocks to cover the large hole.

The limousine that carried Lafonza Viatsi and his men drove away into the darkness of the night.

46

AFTER Three DAYS of an intense search for any survivors, the search was called off.

As much as Katherine wanted Cole and Justin to be found, the miracle she had hoped for was slowly fading away. She closed her eyes and remembered happier times when the phone broke the silence. "Hello, Katherine Wentworth."

"Miss Wentworth, my name is, Kyle Chambers. I worked with Cole in security on the island project."

"Yes, I met you once. What can I do for you, Mr. Chambers?"

"Well, ma'am, I just found a tape from a security camera that filmed the blast. It had some interesting footage on it."

"Tell me some good news, Kyle. I really need it right now." She closed her eyes and rubbed her forehead.

"That's just it, Miss Wentworth. I don't know what it is but I wanted to show you to see what you thought."

"Where are you at, Kyle?"

"I'm downstairs at the security desk. The guard won't let me through."

"Hand the phone to him and then come up to the twentieth floor. I'll meet you at the elevator."

A few minutes later, Kyle came up and immediately showed her the tape.

Kyle stopped the tape at one point, "There!"

"I see two blurry streaks," Katherine said.

"But I believe the two streaks could be Cole and Justin running. It's a long shot, but if they could have made it out of the hotel, there's a hurricane shelter right where the streaks disappear."

"Wait a minute. You're right! The shelter has a big steel top on it and would have shielded them from the blast. My God, Kyle! They would be buried under so much debris that no one could ever find them. Not even the FBI dogs that combed the area. The steel door would seal the smell and the dogs could never find them."

"It's a long shot, ma'am, but I had to run it by you."

"If this is true, we need to get to them quickly or they will die."

"They've been in there for three days now. We don't have much time left."

Katherine made a few phone calls and she and Kyle got in the helicopter and took off towards the island. She brought water and snack food in case they found them.

Kyle brought maps of the island and the hotel so they could pinpoint exactly where to dig.

Forty minutes later, they landed on the island still filled with debris. Both of them ran towards the spot where they thought the shelter was.

"Kyle, I can't make heads or tails out of this mess." Katherine looked around frantically.

"Let's lay out the map and find out where we are." He found a flat piece of concrete to lay the map on.

When they both agreed on a general area, they waited for the equipment to arrive. After several impatient phone calls from Katherine, the equipment finally arrived and it seemed to take an eternity to start digging.

After two hours with no success, Katherine and Kyle went back to the map. They knew about where the shelter was but it was still only a guess.

Two more hours passed and there was still no sign of the shelter.

Katherine ran her hand through her hair and looked at Kyle. "You know even if we don't find these guys, I'd like to thank you for coming to me with this. I want you to come to work for me, Kyle."

"Really? Doing what?" He asked.

"Head of security. When I'm elected as the next senator of Texas I'll need good security people to protect me."

"I'd be honored, ma'am." He smiled at her.

"No matter how this turns out, thank you for giving me new hope."

"I want this to turn out good for everyone. But it's a long shot and we have to keep that in mind."

"Well, Kyle, my whole life has been a long shot and I somehow still believe that we'll find them."

"Hey over here!" one of the workers yelled.

Katherine and Kyle ran towards the man. They finally saw the steel door they had looked for so long.

"Oh my God! That's it!" Katherine yelled.

"Get some pry bars to open this thing up!" Kyle said as he jumped down into the hole.

Two workers jumped down with pry bars and several people gathered around the hole.

Katherine said a silent prayer as the men worked to get the door open. It seemed to take forever, but finally it opened.

The silence was soon broken when Justin's dirty face smiled at everyone. They all cheered as he showed himself. Katherine broke out in tears when she saw him and she hugged her brother when he was lifted up.

He hugged her back and took a drink of water.

"Justin, thank god we found you! Is Cole with you?" She had tears in her eyes.

"Well, I didn't go back in that hotel for souvenirs. Just your cowboy." He said taking another hit from the jug of water.

Katherine looked down into the hole and saw Cole's dirty face smiling at her. "Oh my god, Cole!" She stretched her arms out toward him as he was raised from the hole. She hugged and kissed him hoping it wasn't a dream.

"Justin broke my hands free just before the explosion. We ran to the shelter but I didn't know if we would ever be found under all that concrete." Cole was covered with dirt.

"I can't believe you're really here." Tears streamed down Katherine's cheeks.

"How did you ever know to look for us down there?" Cole took a drink of water.

"It was a long shot that paid off." Kyle looked at Katherine.

"Thank you, Kyle. I'll never be able to repay you for this." She smiled and cried at the same time.

"Well, if that security job is still open that would work. We make a pretty good team." Kyle smiled at her.

"You're hired." Katherine kissed him on the cheek.

"I'll settle for a handshake, Kyle. Thanks, buddy," Cole shook his hand.

The paramedics checked out Cole and Justin.

When Cole was done with the paramedics, he looked at Katherine. "I can't believe your hotel is gone."

Katherine smiled at him. "I have a confession to make, Cole. The whole idea of building this hotel was all a well orchestrated lie. I had to make it look believable so my father wouldn't find out what I was really building.

Cole blew out a breath. "I'll never understand why you Texans have to do everything on such a grand scale. It took all of these perfect lies to fool your father. I guess you out smarted him at his own game. So where is your other project?" He asked.

"The Yellow Rose Hotel and Casino on the Las Vegas strip."

"Normally, Katherine, I would be shocked. But with you, I know better. So what now?"

"Well, I plan to become the next senator of Texas."

"Why doesn't that surprise me either? What about your hotel in Las Vegas?" He held her hand.

"I'm going to ask Justin to run it."

"I'm starved; can we get something to eat?" Cole asked.

"I thought we might fly to Vegas and I'll show you my hotel. I have a wonderful penthouse that faces the East and the view of the sunrise is spectacular."

"Really? I've been known to enjoy a sunrise or two." He smiled at her. "Tell me, do we take Martin's word that we aren't related?"

"His word wasn't good enough for me. I had blood drawn and tested while he was in custody."

"And?"

"Let's just say you may not see any sunrises for a few days. You'll be busy."

"That place of yours have room service?" He asked. "Of course it does."

"Good. I haven't eaten anything for five days and I don't want to leave the room that much. It sounds like I'll need all my strength."

Katherine smiled at him, “I’ll take good care of you, Cole.”

www.ingramcontent.com/pod-product-compliance
Lightning Source LLC
LaVergne TN
LVHW020536100826
845148LV00010B/1489

* 9 7 8 0 9 8 4 1 7 0 1 0 4 *